Greenfield
for
President

Greenfield

for

President

Arthur D. Robbins

ACROPOLIS BOOKS
New York

Publisher's-Cataloging in Publication Data

Robbins, Arthur D.
Greenfield for President /by Arthur D. Robbins
p.   cm.
ISBN 0-9676127-5-6
I. Title.
$PS_{3568} \cdot O_{22}$ 2001
813.0876—dc21   99-76122

Published by Acropolis Books P.O. Box 2629 New York, NY 10009

Printed in the United States of America
First Edition
TS 10 9 8 7 6 5 4 3 2 1

BOOK DESIGN BY GLEN M.EDELSTEIN

To my coach, my mentor,
and my most severe critic:
My son, Matthew

ACKNOWLEDGMENTS

Most authors have a single editor. I have been fortunate enough to have many, to each of whom I express my deepest gratitude:

Bob Bachner, Ann Close, Henry Ferris, James Furino, Deborah Grifffin, Joel Hochman, Phyllis Kahn, Pat Mulcahy, Larry Ratzkin, Matthew Robbins, Jill Sieracki, Kim Caldwell Steffen, Joseph Steuer, Liz Vought, Melanie Yolles.

Special thanks to Peg Munves, who could not have been more generous with her time or helpful with her suggestions, and to Grace Epstein, at Acropolis Books, for her support and editorial guidance.

"A lie can go halfway around the world, before the truth even gets its boots on."

—*Mark Twain*

CHAPTER 1

FROM THE TIME HE could speak till the age of five, Jeremiah Greenfield told the truth. He told the truth about writing with crayons on the wallpaper in the hall and about stopping up the toilet in the downstairs bathroom. He was yelled at, spanked and humiliated. By the age of six he noticed that those around him lied – especially his parents – and that they did well for themselves in the process. Jeremiah began testing the waters and found that the sailing was a lot smoother when he lied, too. By the time he was eight he was lying with dedication and conviction, creating things to lie about, confessing to doing things he didn't do.

On the occasion of Jeremiah's ninth birthday there was a party with relatives from both sides of the family. When asked what he wanted to do when he grew up, Jeremiah answered with abject seriousness.

"I want to be a liar like Daddy."

This drew chuckles and guffaws.

"Why don't you run for president, sonny?" asked his grandfather.

"What do you think, Daddy?" asked Jeremiah.

Jeremiah's father was a bookie who parlayed his many connections into a successful career as a politician. As mayor of Paltry, in upstate New York, he presided over one of the most corrupt townships in the county. He siphoned money off the school budget to pay gambling debts. He built a new swimming pool at taxpayers' expense, and restructured the retirement system for town employees in such a way as to enable himself to retire at the age of fifty with a salary of $150,000 per annum.

In private, Saul Greenfield was a falling-down drunk who would beat his son with a rolled-up newspaper as if he were a dog and trained him to respond to commands from the age of six months – "Stay!" "Sit!" "Come!" – which Jeremiah's mother, Hilda, boasted about to the neighbors. Hilda worshiped her husband and insisted that Jeremiah treat his father with the utmost respect. Jeremiah called his father "Sir." He shined his shoes, fluffed his pillows, cleaned up his vomit, and honored him with a ritualistic kiss on his ring finger before going to bed each night.

Saul liked to fish. In the summer, he fished almost every evening after supper. In autumn, he fished till the last leaf had fallen from the trees. At his side was his son Jeremiah. These were the most memorable moments from Jeremiah's childhood. These father-son expeditions lasted a little more than three years. Then Hilda decided they were taking too much time from Jeremiah's schoolwork and threw away his fishing rod.

Wintertime, Saul helped Jeremiah with his stamp collection. Claiming it was an accident, one day Hilda threw away his stamps as she was cleaning out his closet. Whatever mattered most to Jeremiah, Hilda saw to it that it was discarded.

In the fifth grade – shortly after the beginning of the school year – Jeremiah reported to Mrs. Gambol that Bobby Grimes, the best student in the class, had cheated on the history test. Bobby went home with a note. His parents were called into school. Jeremiah admitted that he had made it all up.

"That's it," said Hilda. "You're going to see a therapist."

The logical choice was Dr. Marvin Allworth, the most successful medical practitioner in the town of Paltry, who specialized in doing appendectomies on psychosomatic patients. Allworth was balding and handsome. He had a calming and sympathetic manner, wore glasses – though he could see perfectly well without them – which he would take off once or twice during a consultation for purposes of emphasis, sometimes pointing to a diagram, sometimes sketching on the blackboard, sometimes resorting to a medical tome for further clarification. "The appendix," he would say, "is the least understood and hence the most important organ in the body." From there he would go on to explain how the hypothalamus, "the seat of the emotions, and the motor for all human behavior," derived its milk from all over the body, drawing most heavily on the appendix, which, in psychosomatic patients, due to a genetic defect, was sour. This, he explained, was the problem. Once the source of sour milk was eliminated, the patient would be freed from the psychological disturbances that had been plaguing him for decades. By this point in the conversation, Allworth could charge whatever he wished, which is what he usually did.

For Saul Greenfield, however, there would be no charge, owing to the many favors the mayor had done for him over the years. And the cure would be something altogether different.

"Sit over here," he said to Jeremiah in softly modulated tones, pointing to an oversized leather chair. Allworth pulled up his rolling desk chair to within a foot of Jeremiah.

"Place your left hand on your left knee. Your right hand on your right knee. That's good. Very good. Now just relax." Allworth gazed into Jeremiah's eyes. With his right hand extended to his side, he moved a small penlight in a slow, circular motion.

"Tell me the place you most enjoy being, a place that is just yours, where no one will bother you."

"The tree house in the backyard," said Jeremiah sleepily.

"Good. Very good. Now I want you to imagine yourself in your tree house all by yourself. Think about climbing up the ladder. Imagine how the wood feels. Think of how it smells. Are you there?"

"Yes," said Jeremiah slowly.

"Good," said Allworth. "Now count backwards from ten, one number at a time, after me."

Jeremiah did as instructed.

"You are asleep, Jeremiah," said Allworth. "Can you hear me?"

"Yes," said Jeremiah from afar.

"Good," said Allworth. "Jeremiah, you are in a wonderful place. You are safe. You are at peace. You are filled with a sense of well-being. You are in complete power. No one and nothing can stop you. The world is yours. This is where you will be every time you tell the truth. Do you understand, Jeremiah?"

"Yes," said Jeremiah.

"Now, Jeremiah, I want you to imagine your worst nightmare. Do you have nightmares?"

"Yes," said Jeremiah.

"What is the worst nightmare you have ever had?"

No response.

"Tell me, Jeremiah. Tell me your worst nightmare."

"I am on a stage."

"Continue, Jeremiah."

"There are people from school, students and teachers. The principal is sitting in the middle of the stage in a high throne. He is dressed in rags. He is filthy and disgusting. There is a puddle of vomit. Some students have gotten out of their seats and are staring at the vomit and watching me. 'Now, Jeremiah,' says the principal, 'lick up the vomit. Every bit of it.' Everybody laughs and cheers. The principal gets down off his throne. He is holding a rolled-up newspaper. He beats me with the newspaper. I lick up the vomit. There is cheering and screaming. Everyone is laughing, even the principal."

"Good, Jeremiah. That is a terrible nightmare. That is an awful experience to live through. Every time you lie you will be on that stage licking up the vomit. The principal will be beating you. The students will be laughing and cheering. You cannot escape. When you lie that is where you will be. Do you understand?"

"Yes," said Jeremiah.

"Good," said Allworth. "Every time you lie, Jeremiah, you will wink with your right eye. Everyone will know that you are a liar. You have no control over this wink and will never be able to stop it. Do you understand, Jeremiah?"

"Yes," said Jeremiah.

"Good," said Allworth. "Now I want you count slowly after me, from one to ten. At ten you will be awake. You will forget everything that just happened."

Jeremiah did as instructed and opened his eyes. It seemed as if he had just sat down.

"That's all for today, Jeremiah," said Allworth. "Your mother is waiting outside. Now you are going to be a good boy. Isn't that true?"

"You bet," said Jeremiah, winking with his right eye.

Thus was established in Jeremiah Greenfield at the tender age of nine years the conflict which was to govern his life till the day of his death: to lie or to tell the truth. Each lie would fill him with torment which, over the years, he learned to live with, periodically succumbing to paroxysms of self-contempt. The wink never went away. In his teen years young women thought he was making a pass. Later on people thought it was Tourette's syndrome. Friends and relatives knew he was lying.

CHAPTER 2

IN THE AUTUMN OF his junior year in high school, Jeremiah fell in love. Katelyn lived in a small, gray-shingled house in one of the less prosperous neighborhoods. She was Irish. She was Catholic. Her father was a bricklayer. Hilda forbade Jeremiah from ever being in Katelyn's presence. After all, she wasn't Jewish. Hilda's interdiction only served to intensify the passion which united the two young people. In class, they exchanged furtive glances and passed notes. They held hands on the way home from school and kissed in the dark on wintry nights on the front steps of Katelyn's house when no one was looking. They wrote love letters. Katelyn quoted Byron, Keats and Shelley. Jeremiah poured his heart out. For sure he would marry her and love her till the end of time. One day he came to pick her up on the way to school. No one else was home. She was barefoot in her plaid skirt and Irish-knit sweater. He watched as her unshod, arched foot slipped gracefully into her sock. The moment was filled with longing. The image would never leave him.

Summertime came and they were with each other every day, despite Hilda's best efforts to keep them apart. The second week in August, Katelyn appeared at the door of Jeremiah's house and, braving Hilda's admonishments, insisted on seeing Jeremiah at once. Hilda complied. Looking at her green eyes through the screen door, Jeremiah knew that something awful was about to happen.

"We're going back to Ireland, in September," she said, her eyes swollen with emotion.

Jeremiah saw Katelyn every day for the next three weeks. He traveled all the way to the airport by train and bus. It was the most troubled hour and a half of his life waiting for her plane to take off. He wanted time to stand still so she would never leave. He wanted her to leave at once and relieve him of his anguish. There was one last embrace.

"Jeremiah, you will always be in my heart," she said.

Katelyn turned to wave good-bye and then was gone. Jeremiah watched the plane taxi down the runway. He watched the plane take off and gradually get smaller until it disappeared. There was an invisible cord, one end of which was attached to the plane. The other end was attached to Jeremiah's heart. When the plane disappeared, the cord snapped. Nothing in Jeremiah's life was ever quite right again.

Jeremiah was a bright student. He had gotten good grades in his junior year. After Katelyn left, his grades started slipping. He would get one hundreds on his math and science tests and then barely pass the course for want of homework assignments. He was suspended more than once for carrying on in class. In the last half of his senior year, he was failing half his courses. One day in April, he hit his English teacher in the back of the head with an uncooked egg. He had been aiming for his friend in the first row. Saul Greenfield was called to school. A deal was struck: Jeremiah would graduate on time if he performed community service. Jeremiah spent the last two months of high school recovering paper cups, beer cans, newspapers and stray hubcaps from the side of the local highway. From there he went straight into the army. Jeremiah had no say in the matter.

It is difficult to determine who had the worst of it: Jeremiah or the army. He enjoyed nothing more than provoking authority, regardless of the consequences. His fellow inductees loved him for it and encouraged his misdeeds. The more push-ups he did, the stronger he would get, so Jeremiah counseled himself. He spent a night in the stockade for short-sheeting his sergeant.

In his second year, Jeremiah met Nick Belladonna, the son of a wealthy Park Avenue physician. After a year at Harvard, Nick had decided it was time to get serious. Over his father's objections, he dropped out of school, dusted off the old Leica and started shooting everything from magnolia blossoms to stop signs.

"One more dirty dish in the sink and you are out on your ass," George Belladonna had said to his son.

Nick took him at his word and made a neat stack on the floor, in the corner, near the broom closet. This is not what the old man had in mind.

"I am sure the army could put your talents to good use," he had said. He was right.

Nick's talent as a photographer got him a stint in Communications, where he met Jeremiah, who was working for the base newsletter. They immediately took a liking to each other, did assignments together and spent their time off at the same bars. Nick was a serious drinker and skirt-chaser.

Eventually, Jeremiah even won the friendship of his superior officers. He was a loyal friend, easygoing and playful. He was neither competitive nor vindictive. Granted, he played fast and free with the truth, but no one seemed to care. People saw it as part of his charm.

When he stood tall, Jeremiah measured over six feet. Usually he walked stoop-shouldered, in a slow, ambling gate. He was solid at over two hundred pounds, largely from all of those push-ups. Women found his thick brown hair and warm smile appealing, especially one Emma Fink, daughter of the largest clothing-store owner in Smytheville, Pennsylvania, a town fifteen minutes from the base.

Emma was a large-breasted, voluminous woman, who immediately established proprietorship over Jeremiah. She was crass, slovenly and self-indulgent with little talent but a businessman's sense of the worth of a dollar. She was not easily fooled. She was not easily cowed. She was what she appeared to be and nothing else.

"Be careful," Nick had warned.

"Don't worry, I know what I'm doing," said Jeremiah. Clearly, he didn't.

The couple married a week before Jeremiah's discharge. Just about everybody on the base joined in the celebration. Just about everybody knew Jeremiah was making the mistake of his life. No one could explain why he was doing it, least of all Jeremiah.

CHAPTER 3

EMMA'S FATHER, BERNIE FINK, was a businessman to his bones. He had a hairy chest and wore a gold chain, both of which were visible through his open shirt collar. He wore a large ring on the fourth finger of his left hand. He smoked cigars and was an avid golfer. He started out as the owner of a modest one-thousand-square-foot shop, selling dungarees and work shirts to men. By the time Jeremiah married into the family, Bernie had a thirty-thousand-square-foot establishment, on two floors, selling designer clothes to men and women.

Bernie gave the newlyweds the down payment for an impressive home in the right part of town. He bought them a second-hand Buick and a brand new lawn mower. He was going to teach Jeremiah the business from the ground up and then pass it on to him when he was ready for retirement. Without meaning to, Jeremiah had married the boss's daughter.

Jeremiah started out in purchasing. It was his job to purchase everything from paper clips and hangers to bathroom supplies and light bulbs. Jeremiah ordered too much of this and not enough of that. Some things he forgot to order altogether. Bernie decided to switch him to the floor. Jeremiah was good with customers but could never get the knack of writing up a sales slip or getting the right size shirt or jacket for his customers. Bernie was starting to have second thoughts.

Smytheville, Pennsylvania, is a town of some thirty thousand suburban home-dwellers. Main Street – its proud architecture going back to the mid-eighteen hundreds – had become a hangout for drug dealers and vagrants. It was unsafe to visit the few remaining restaurants and bars after dark. Suburban sprawl had sapped the town of its soul.

Smytheville social life was divided along strict class lines. At the top of the pecking order were the physicians. To be invited into one of their homes at holiday time was the highest honor this small-town society had to offer. The neighborhood one lived in, the color and texture of the grass on one's front lawn, the size and shape of one's back deck, the presence or absence of a swimming pool, where and how often one vacationed, all these factors taken cumulatively determined just how much social mobility one would be accorded.

Jeremiah could not have been more unhappy. Wealth and status meant nothing to him. He was not much of a golfer and found the exchange of dinner invitations with these self-satisfied middle-class gentry tedious. Emma, on the other hand, could not have been happier. She had a husband. She had a home and – thanks to her father – enough money to acquire the status she sought. She had no children and never intended having any. This she had made clear to Jeremiah when they first met. She had no career and no wish to work. After all, she was a married woman.

Emma sensed that Jeremiah was out of place and quickly losing interest in the life she so dearly prized.

"Why don't you get into politics?" she suggested.

This was not a bad idea. It fit in very nicely with the vision

Jeremiah had for himself, a vision no less grand, and perhaps more so, than the one which Emma had for herself. Jeremiah Greenfield intended one day to be president of the United States.

Some would call it a quirk, some an obsession, still others a delusion. Everyone teased him about it as they did his wink. Yet ever since that session with Dr. Allworth, Jeremiah had gotten it into his head that he would one day be president. "You are in complete power. You rule. No one and nothing can stop you."

Jeremiah believed in himself as president. He had no doubt that he would one day be elected. Evenings and weekends, he did everything he could to prepare himself for his eventual candidacy.

There were campaign posters, stacks and stacks of them, that one had to walk over and around to get in and out of his bedroom. Emma was very tolerant this way. She actually gave him the money he needed to have professional photographs taken and posters printed, and would even discuss with him, in her practical way, what she thought were the drawbacks or advantages of a particular poster.

Jeremiah wrote speeches. He wrote speeches for times of celebration and times of crisis, speeches honoring those who died for their country going back to the war of independence, speeches honoring bankers, stock brokers and oil executives. And he even wrote speeches honoring elected officials, the hardest job of all.

Jeremiah pondered the various political possibilities in Smytheville and realized that the most intelligent choice was to run for the state assembly. The dentist who had held the seat in his district was running for attorney general. Here was an opportunity made to order. With his father-in-law's influence and Jeremiah's personality he had no trouble getting his name on the ballot and winning the slot for his party. The opposing party offered up a sleepy-eyed dealer in scrap metal. Election time came and Jeremiah was prepared. He knew what the voters· wanted and told them what they wanted to hear. And so they voted him in. He did a lot of winking that year.

There was one subject about which Jeremiah could not lie: the environment. He had a strong attachment to those streams and lakes where he had spent so many contented moments fishing with his father. In his first term he began a campaign to clean up the waters. Ecoline Transistor, the largest industrial polluter in his county, was his target. It was Jeremiah's goal to pass legislation prohibiting further pollution. He was close to realizing his goal and was up for reelection. Ecoline mounted a strenuous public relations campaign against Jeremiah. It spread rumors that he cheated on his taxes and on his wife. Company officials let it be known that if this legislation were passed they would be shutting their doors and moving to another part of the country. That's all it took to convince the voters that Jeremiah was up to no good. The scrap metal dealer was a shoo-in.

About six months later — he had just celebrated his thirty-third birthday — Jeremiah received another jolt when Bernie Fink decided to sell the business and retire to Florida. No amount of pleading on Emma's part could convince her father that Jeremiah could take over. Jeremiah did not even bother trying.

At the age of thirty-three Jeremiah was being called upon to support himself and Emma. He had no career. It never even crossed his mind to choose one. Earning money simply had never been one of his concerns.

Emma was by turns morbidly depressed and viciously aggressive. She had had everything she wanted. And now it was all slipping through her fingers. She held Jeremiah fully accountable and would never forgive him.

The last thing Emma wanted to do was leave Smytheville. But, under the circumstances, she realized it was the wisest choice. No matter what happened, Jeremiah would never be able to support her in the style to which she had been accustomed. She would never be able to hold her head up amongst her peers. The only choice was to leave. This is what Jeremiah had wanted all along, which made it doubly painful for Emma. Not only did he ruin her life but now he was getting his way. They both agreed on New York City as the next destination. Opportunities abounded. Even someone like Jeremiah would find a place for himself. Bernie said he would use his connections to get Jeremiah started.

CHAPTER 4

THE COUPLE FOUND AN inexpensive walk-up apartment in Manhattan's East Village. Under Emma's guidance and her father's influence, Jeremiah was hired as a manager of a discount shoe store on Fourteenth Street. Jeremiah knew nothing about shoes or management. At the end of three months he was fired. Emma met a woman who made her living selling display ads for Times Square bulletin boards. She convinced her to take Jeremiah on as an assistant. Jeremiah disliked Estelle on sight. Next, Emma managed to line up a job with a fabric shop on Orchard Street.

"I am going to get a job waiting on tables," said Jeremiah.

"No, you are not," said Emma.

On this Jeremiah did not yield.

For a little more than a year, Jeremiah worked at Giacomos, an old-fashioned Italian restaurant in lower Manhattan. At the end of six months he realized that his future lay elsewhere. At the end of a year, he became desperate but could think of no alternative.

"Will today be another day just like the last?" he would ask himself each morning. "Definitely not" was the persistent reply. This day would be different.

Jeremiah would begin the day looking for omens to prove to himself that he was right. Omens were small occurrences, usually misadventures and annoying inconveniences, that Jeremiah took as proof that his luck was about to change.

He would awake with a headache. That was a good sign. He would nick himself shaving. Another good sign. He could tell by the aroma coming from the kitchen that today Emma had baked zucchini bread, his least favorite. These were all good signs. And when he got to work, if his boss told him he would have to work a double shift this was proof positive that something important was going to happen. Yet nothing ever did.

One day, a heavy, brown mist blanketed the city. The temperature had not dropped below sixty-five degrees in more than a week. Piles of heavy, winter coats could be seen on many a street corner, discarded like so many crippled umbrellas after a windy storm. Rats scurried from one garbage can to the next in broad daylight. It was mid-January in Manhattan, in the year 2002.

It was after eleven, and close to closing time. Jeremiah was heading back towards the restaurant kitchen when a voice called after him.

"I asked for spaghetti and meat balls," whined a heavyset woman in her sixties, with short, frizzy red hair.

"I'm sorry," said Jeremiah, bending over the table in an act of solicitousness, "but we are all out of spaghetti and meat balls. The *tagliatelle bolognese* is the house specialty."

"But I asked for spaghetti and meat balls," said the woman, with shrillness in her voice this time.

Jeremiah, his large frame in a slouch, raised his eyebrows, shrugged his shoulders and picked up the plate.

"I'll have the check," said a man hidden from sight in a corner booth on the far side of the restaurant. This was not one of Jeremiah's tables. Jeremiah put down the plate of pasta.

"I'm sorry," he began, looking through his pad of checks just to make sure. He looked up. It was none other than Nick Belladonna.

"Nick," he said.

"Jeremiah," came back the reply.

The two men had lost track of each other after Jeremiah had gotten married. They had met once for drinks after Nick found a newspaper job and on occasion after that when Jeremiah visited New York. It had been years since they had been in contact. Jeremiah brought Nick up to date on his life in Smytheville and his career in politics. Nick talked about his job at the *Ledger*. They reminisced about army days.

Jeremiah got himself a glass. Nick poured wine into Jeremiah's glass and refilled his own.

"To Sergeant Kastavian, the lousy bastard," said Nick.

"To Sergeant Kastavian."

Nick poured some more wine into his glass, swirled it around and then gulped it down.

"You can do better than this," Nick said, nodding in the direction of "spaghetti lady," as he referred to her. "Call me tomorrow afternoon. I'll see if I can set something up."

"Thanks, Nick," said Jeremiah.

"I'll be waiting for your call," said Nick as he got up to leave.

Jeremiah had written for his high school newspaper and the army base newsletter but had never considered a career in journalism. Yet almost at once it seemed that writing newspaper stories had been his calling all along. He couldn't wait to get home and tell Emma about his meeting with Nick.

"Guess what?" he said, taking off his coat and throwing it on the sofa.

"You should really hang that up," said Emma.

Dutifully, Jeremiah picked up his coat, passing along the day's news with his head buried in the closet.

"I can't hear a word you said," said Emma, taking a bite out of a Ben and Jerry's Cherry Garcia frozen yogurt on a stick.

"Guess who I met today?"

"I can't imagine," she said.

"Nick Belladonna," he said.

"Oh," said Emma coolly. Emma did not like Nick.

"Guess what else," he said, turning off the television.

"You shouldn't do that," she said.

"Nick works for a paper in New Jersey. He thinks he can get me on as a reporter."

"Where the hell is New Jersey?" asked Emma. "And why would anyone want to hire you as reporter?"

"Don't you see what this means? This might actually lead to something. A career. Who knows? Anything is possible."

Emma was starting to see dollar signs.

"You know," she said, placing one of the throw pillows on her lap, "if you play your cards right, you can move from print to the six o'clock news and I can be looking at your smirking face instead of one of those other jerks."

This was not what Jeremiah had in mind.

"It's not about money," said Jeremiah, sitting down on the couch beside Emma. "It's about something bigger. It's about the truth."

Like Jeremiah, Emma was a liar. In her case, however, there was no turmoil. There was no winking. It was in response to Emma's lying and more out of rebellion than conviction that, early on in their marriage, Jeremiah began developing an interest in the truth. Or was it once again that session with Allworth and the tree house?

"*Liebling*," said Emma, taking his hand, "people don't want the truth. They want to be entertained."

"The elections, the vote, the entire system is a scam," said Jeremiah.

"No one cares," said Emma.

"The truth," said Jeremiah, reclaiming his hand, "will save the world."

"And what," said Emma, rising from the couch to turn on the television, "will save us? Look at you, Mr. Has Been and future president of the United States, waiting on tables in a cheap Italian restaurant on the Lower East Side. If not for the money Papa is sending us we couldn't even afford this flea trap," she said, turning up the volume.

"It is not 'the Lower East Side,'" said Jeremiah, straining to talk over the television. "It is in an area of town known as 'Noho,' which stands for 'North of Houston.' And further, it is not a 'cheap Italian restaurant.' It is a restaurant with pride and tradition, which has been serving homemade pasta to discriminating diners for the past seventy-five years."

"Oh," said Emma. "I didn't know."

"And," said Jeremiah, knocking a magazine off the coffee table, "do not make light of my presidential ambitions."

"You should pick that up," said Emma, pointing to the magazine.

"I am going out to take a walk," said Jeremiah, ignoring Emma's entreaty.

CHAPTER 5

THE NEXT DAY JEREMIAH called Nick and that was the beginning of his career as a reporter for the *North Benware Star Ledger*, the only paper he ever worked for. Originally owned by a family of media moguls, the paper was bought at auction by Maynard E. Brown, who is black, and his wife Sissy Black, who is white. They got it for a song.

The *Ledger* is a small suburban newspaper across the Hudson that has pretensions, and sometimes lives up to them, of being more than just another local rag. The paper has its offices in a three-story stone building that had once served as the post office. The building, close to 150 years old, is a town landmark. The previous owners of the *Ledger* established it as the home of the town's only paper. Production is on the first floor, Editorial on the second.

Nick met Jeremiah at the main entrance, gave him a tour of the plant and then accompanied him to the second floor. On the

perimeter of the large open space were separate offices with identifying titles on the doors. Most prominent was the office of the
"Publisher and Managing Editor," Maynard E. Brown. Immediately
to the right was a much smaller, untitled office. Reading a book,
her feet atop the desk, was Sissy Black. Sensing Jeremiah's presence,
she put down her book and rose to greet him. About five feet ten
inches tall, with a slender face, high cheekbones, light brown shoul-
der-length hair and dressed in a pair of cashmere slacks and a loose-
fitting, white linen blouse, she was strikingly attractive. Jeremiah
introduced himself. Sissy replied with a firm handshake and a
friendly smile.

"Nick has told me a lot about you," she said. "I think you might
be an interesting addition to the staff. I hope you understand,
though, that much of the work is routine. Yet, who knows, someone
with talent might turn this job into something extraordinary."

"I think I have a sense of what Americans want," replied Jeremiah.

"Good," said Sissy, a little taken aback.

Accompanying him to the adjoining office, Sissy introduced
Jeremiah to Maynard, who offered him a most hearty, salesman-like
greeting.

"Jeremiah," he said, not letting go of Jeremiah's hand, "We are
lucky to have you with us and you are lucky to be here. Some of our
brethren see us as just another small-town operation. And that is
where they are wrong. In five years or less we will have a national
following and the attention of the highest elected officials in this
country. You can count on that," he said, finally letting go of
Jeremiah's hand.

Maynard, who was turned down at Yale, graduated summa cum
laude from Harvard. Women found him irresistible, especially white
women. He was a magnificent physical specimen, quick with a
smile, thoughtful to a fault and unbelievably ambitious. In fact, if
not for his coal black skin no one ever would have guessed he was
black, so white he was. Here was a man who was perfection, and
he was black and he was married to white money. That was the
kicker. Sissy came from old money, via Oyster Bay, and when she

married Maynard her father cut her off with $30 million, on which she had been limping along ever since.

Nick reappeared and led Jeremiah to a far corner of the office where there was a desk near a window.

"Well, what do you think?" Nick asked.

"Not bad," said Jeremiah.

He spent the rest of the day going over old newspapers and learning something about North Benware, a wealthy community in northern New Jersey, which had once been part of a thousand-acre estate owned by a man named Alfred E. Benware. Of the original architecture only the gatehouse remained. It was occupied by descendants of Alfred E. who were influential in local politics.

The next day the job began in earnest. Most of the time was spent in filling out forms and sharpening pencils. People were too busy to give Jeremiah the direction he needed. However, by the end of the second week, he printed his first story for the *Ledger*. Gradually he settled into a routine, turning out stories on a weekly basis, covering anything from funerals to high-society social events. With great ease he adapted himself to the world of gossip and irrelevancy. There were masked balls, debutante balls, Fourth of July extravaganzas, and costumed Halloween parties about which the besotted and crapulent expected to read, in detail, in the morning paper. Jeremiah attended these events regularly, with Nick at his side photographing ice sculpture, bare backs and bodices. Jeremiah had a knack for winning the trust of unsuspecting revelers who would read their uncensored remarks over coffee the following morning. Maynard was quite impressed.

One day, after Jeremiah had been with the paper for close to a year, Maynard called him into his office.

"Jeremiah," he said, swiveling in his desk chair from one side to the other, "our future is in Washington. We need someone who can penetrate into the darkest, hidden recesses of national affairs. Someone who will let our readers in on how this democracy of ours functions when no one is looking."

"I'd like to give it a try," said Jeremiah.

"Good," said Maynard. "Book yourself a flight to Washington and let's see what you can come up with. Here's a list of contacts."

Jeremiah spent the next few days on the telephone. The following Monday he was on a plane bound for the nation's capital. But the assignment was not going to be as easy as he thought it would be.

Washington gives the impression of being an open town. There is an easy intermingling of senators, congressmen, reporters and White House staff to which anyone walking in off the street has access if he knows which pub or restaurant is the current favorite. People are friendly and easy to talk to but difficult to engage in serious conversation on subjects of controversy. The sparring that erupts every so often during television interviews, especially at election time, is no different than what takes place during a televised wrestling match. One opponent slams the other to the mat while the cameras are on and then goes out drinking with him till the early hours of the morning when the cameras are off. Jeremiah ticked off every name on Maynard's list but was getting nowhere. He would have to find other resources if he were to penetrate the secrets of Washington political life. And that is just what he did.

At the beginning of January 2003, the head of the FBI resigned under suspicious circumstances. A week later a second-level cabinet member swallowed arsenic after being caught shoplifting at the local K-mart. Jeremiah and Nick were on hand to cover the funeral.

The funeral parlor was filled with politicos and hangers-on. The House, the Senate, the Justice Department, the President's Office, and the National Security Council were represented. There were deacons, ministers, priests, rabbis and a cardinal or two. There were mafia and Latin American drug dealers. There was an array of women, some of them respectable looking, some of them not so. The usual Washington mix.

There was a lot of chatter. Everyone seemed to have something to say about Smelly Fisch. It's not too often in Washington that someone's sense of honor drives him to suicide. There were different versions of what really happened. There was talk that Smelly had a brain tumor, that he was murdered because he knew too much, that his wife refused to divorce him and that he needed a way out. It was probably all true, or none of it.

All of a sudden things got quiet. The minister, a slight, gaunt man in his mid-sixties made his way to the podium and was getting ready to speak. He arranged some papers, adjusted his Adam's apple and then began. Like Jeremiah he had a twitch on the right side of his face.

After the usual religious intonings, there was a eulogy.

"A light has gone out," said Reverend Gideon Jones, his voice fading. "A light has gone out. The horizon is dimmer and the cost of electricity continues to rise. Smelly Fisch has passed on to another life, leaving behind a trail of errors and misdeeds, both heinous and trivial, for us to remember him by."

The minister paused, his eyes drifting across the rows of mourners, stopping here and there on the visage of a key figure in Smelly's life, just to let that person know that he knew what that person must be going through.

"A smudge on the family escutcheon, a blight on the administration which he served with feckless devotion, he will be remembered by friend and foe alike as petty, self-serving and corrupt. He will be missed by a wife" – Gideon glanced her way. She returned his look with one of her own – "whom he betrayed countless times, and a list of mistresses" – here he paused to survey the row of past-their-prime overdressed women in the front of the chapel – "as long as your arm to each of whom he promised uncompromising devotion before passing on to the next.

"But," he said, pointing a finger heavenward, "let not he who lives in a suburban home with picture windows cast the first stone. For all of us given the opportunity and the deceased's lack of character would have done likewise."

He paused, winked and swallowed as he began his crescendo.

"Can anyone here – other than myself – lay claim to honesty and integrity? Can anyone – and I am speaking especially to the many government representatives I see in this crowded room – deny having lied and cheated, accepted bribes and other emoluments?"

No one rose to claim the prize.

"Is there anyone here who hasn't disgraced himself in the public eye? Then let us not be harsh on poor Smelly, who took his own life rather than face a jail sentence for shoplifting.

"And what was it this desperate fellow took on that fateful day? A pair of black, lace panties. Is there any man here – myself excluded – who hasn't done the same thing many times – and has simply been fortunate enough to have escaped detection?"

The minister winked and continued.

"No, my friends, let's not judge Smelly Fisch too harshly, lest we judge ourselves with equal contempt. For we are all of us weak and corrupt and one day might have to pay a similar price.

"No," he said, "let us remember Smelly as he would have wanted us to, sitting on the front porch of his extravagant home in suburban Maryland, sipping on a mint julep while reading soft porn to the strains of Montivanni. That is the way he would have liked it."

The minister dropped his head in worshipful silence, signaling an end to the ceremony. Seated next to Jeremiah was a homely young woman who bit her nails during the entire service. As everyone was getting up to leave, she turned to Jeremiah and, with a tear in the corner of one eye, said, "He was a good man."

"You knew him?" asked Jeremiah, askance, getting a whiff of her breath.

"I was his secretary," she said wistfully.

"Oh," said Jeremiah, rolling his eyes Nick's way, "how interesting."

"Five years. I worked for him for five years," she said, finally breaking down into pathetic sniffling sobs, her face twisted in grief.

"He gave me this," she blubbered.

Jeremiah feigned interest in the cheap trinket she showed him and half listened to her prattle about what it was like to work for the "Distinguished Gentleman," omitting no detail of his daily routine: what time he got out of bed in the morning, what kind of aftershave he used, the tonics, salves and ointments with which he tried to grow a few hairs on his totally hairless head.

"Here," she said, handing Jeremiah a picture of herself with the "Distinguished Gentleman," pointing to the inscription, "To Dorothea Wilson: For Her Hard Work and Devotion. Smelly Fisch."

Dorothea turned to greet one of her secretary friends, a frantic-looking woman with buck teeth and an ashen, dried prune of a face. Taking advantage of this opportunity, Nick and Jeremiah made their getaway, ducking and weaving their way into the crowd. Absent-mindedly, Jeremiah pocketed the photograph. When Dorothea turned to resume her soliloquy, they were long gone.

At home that night Jeremiah emptied his pockets. There was Dorothea's autographed picture. He was about to throw it away when he had second thoughts. He recalled their conversation about Smelly's salves and ointments. Wasn't Dorothea, in fact, a gold mine of the kind of inside information he was after? And weren't there other homely secretaries, like the one she was speaking to at the funeral? And couldn't they be organized into a network of informants who would pass on to him more data than he would know what to do with? The answer to all three questions was yes. And so Jeremiah created the opportunity he was looking for.

Jeremiah wasted no time putting his plan into action. As soon as he got back to the office the next morning he called Ms. Wilson. He apologized for walking off with her photo, explained that he was a reporter, that he had found her conversation very interesting and that he would like to meet with her late this afternoon, if that were possible. Dorothea gladly accepted.

They met at a pizza parlor in downtown Washington, known as Crispy's, a hangout for secretaries on lunch break. Jeremiah was very solicitous.

"Dorothea," he began, once they had found themselves a table, "as I explained over the phone, I am a reporter."

Dorothea nodded.

"A reporter writes a story that gets printed in a newspaper under his name. But where do you think he gets his inside information? How does he know so much?"

"I don't know," she said tentatively, rubbing her finger across her eyebrow as she looked away. "Maybe he has friends," she said, almost in a whisper. "People who know people."

"Exactly," said Jeremiah. "People who know people. People like you."

Here her face lit up.

Jeremiah then went on to explain his plan for developing a network of secretaries who would be his inside sources. As he had predicted, Dorothea couldn't have been more flattered and accepted the assignment of introducing him to the many secretaries she knew. Based on this initial contact and with Dorothea's invaluable assistance, Jeremiah succeeded in meeting, over the ensuing weeks, more than a dozen homely secretaries.

At the end of six months, he had a steady flow of information to draw on. Eventually no one could out-scoop him. He became an expert on matters presidential. There was no aspect of the president's daily routine, no personal habit too insignificant, no occurrence too small or banal, but that Jeremiah Greenfield knew about it and had it documented on the five gigabyte hard drive of his IBM laptop. Readers could not get enough.

Jeremiah knew everything. He knew what the president swallowed, when he swallowed it and how often he chewed. He knew the president's favorite foods, had categorized them by size, color, food group and frequency of use, and could describe, blindfolded and with cotton in his ears, the time of day and setting when another reporter would name the food the president was eating. He knew the president's favorite ice cream flavor, his favorite color, his favorite flower and his favorite curse word, "goshdarn."

CHAPTER 6

June 2003

IT WAS WITH SOME hesitation that Jeremiah submitted the ludicrous story that brought him national recognition for the first time. In January of 2003, the president had confided to reporters that he expected his cabinet to adhere to the "highest ethical standards." By April of the same year he was diverting $10 billion worth of funds – funds allocated for the rehabilitation of the nation's dilapidated schools – to prop up a crumbling dictatorship in what was once Soviet Russia. No one seemed to care. But when Jeremiah came out with his "Blue Tie" story on Sunday, June 9, the effect was explosive.

On Monday, June 10, at 1:00 P.M., the president was to deliver his famous address at a town meeting in Euphoria, Illinois, on the importance of morality in a democratic society. The speech was to be broadcast live around the country and excerpted on major television network evening news broadcasts. Thanks to Jeremiah and one of his inside connections, the *Ledger* readers knew ahead of time that the president would be wearing a "solid blue tie."

Nick was in the office when Maynard got the call from Jeremiah. Maynard couldn't believe his ears.

"I can't believe my ears: a solid blue tie," Maynard said, covering the mouthpiece to the telephone and shouting orders to Meryl, his top assistant.

"Lead story. Upper right. Hold it."

"If this story is what I think it is," said Maynard returning to Jeremiah, "it might be the first step onto the editorial board for you and a lot of money for all of us."

Jeremiah was to get on the next plane back to Newark. A limousine – the paper would pay for it – would be waiting to get him back to the office so he and Maynard could do rewrites, even if it took all night.

"Don't tell anyone about this," Maynard, said before hanging up, "not your wife, your rabbi or your analyst. This is too big to risk losing."

That's how it all began. The morning edition of the *North Benware Star Ledger* sold out before it hit the stands. People were ripping it out of the hands of frightened delivery boys, were stealing it off front stoops and off the backs of trucks. Police barricades were set up outside the stone building on Avarice Street where the paper has its offices. A crowd of about a thousand or so had gathered by 9:00 A.M. chanting Jeremiah's name. There was some pushing and shoving. A few panes of glass were shattered. The situation was volatile. Something had to been done.

"What do you think?" asked Jeremiah, turning to Nick.

"They want you," Nick said. "Why not give them what they want?"

Rising slowly from his chair, Jeremiah walked over to the window. He looked down at the crowd of beseeching eyes turned up at the very window he was looking through, eyes searching for the answer to the riddle of life's misery and meanness. He, Jeremiah

Greenfield, would set things right, make these poor souls feel at home in their own bodies and secure in the world. He could do it with his presence, with a nod, with a word. He opened the French doors, stepped out onto the narrow balcony and was greeted with a roar of voices. People waved frantically.

Jeremiah raised his hand to wipe his brow and the crowd roared. He dropped his hand to his side and the crowd roared. He gave a limp wave of his right hand, as he had seen Margaret Thatcher do when she came to visit the poor of Wall Street. He took both arms, bent at the elbows and raised them as he had once seen a surgeon do and as he had seen the Pope do at St. Peter's square. He extended his stiff right arm in a Hitleresque gesture. The crowd roared. Jeremiah gave one last wave and returned inside. The crowd began to break up. Wistfully people looked back at the balcony where Jeremiah had been standing and then slowly returned home, filled with a renewed sense of purpose in life and a revitalized belief in all that America stood for.

Everyone at the *Ledger* knew he had just witnessed a moment in journalistic history. Maynard was almost reverential in his praise of Jeremiah. He was overcome with gratitude, but most of all greed. He wanted to make sure Jeremiah didn't look for more fertile fields. Ceremoniously he rapped on the desk with his coffee mug. His deep, rich voice quivered slightly as he spoke.

"Jeremiah," he said, "we are proud of you."

Applause and cat whistles.

"You have done what few men ever dare to do."

Pause.

"You have searched for the truth, undaunted by threats of recrimination. A lone voice, singing off pitch in a cacophony of lies, you have given Americans the strength they need to endure a reality so repulsive and distasteful to the human soul, so repugnant to men and women of all ages, races, colors and creeds, that they would rather do anything, even work for a living, than face it."

There was sniffling, nose blowing, a wiping of eyes, a clearing of throats.

Jeremiah, his head bent in worship, looked up when Maynard had finished and said, in a low monotone:

"I am honored, but I never could have done this alone. In fact, I didn't. Without ... without ..."

What Jeremiah almost said, but never did, was, "Without the help of one homely secretary I never would have been standing before you as I now am, filled with pride for what I have accomplished and humiliation for the triviality of what it represents. Of all the inanity which has been offered for truth, this latest caper of mine takes the cake."

In the span of three weeks following Jeremiah's "Blue Tie" story, circulation at the *North Benware Star Ledger* doubled. His Washington trivia started taking over a larger and larger portion of the front page. The paper ran a full story on the president's smile, describing in detail the shape of his smiling mouth, analyzing its frequency of occurrence, comparing it to other smiles in the White House, discussing its history over the course of the president's life, and revealing for the first time that the president had false teeth. This shocked, fascinated and outraged readers who sent many letters of indignation to the editor, complaining that the story was lacking in sufficient detail. They wanted to know if all his teeth were false or just the molars and incisors. They wanted to know what his false teeth were made of, how often he had them cleaned, who did the cleaning. They wanted to know if there was any other part that was false or, for that matter, if there was any part that was real.

But just when all seemed for the best in the best of all possible worlds, things took a turn for the worse. Rumor had gotten around in Washington press circles that the president was very upset about the leaks in the White House pipeline, which was supposed to travel uninterrupted in a perfect circle leading nowhere and signifying nothing. He was especially upset about the "Blue Tie" story. There had been lengthy meetings with his wardrobe advisors. He had brought in outside consultants and had even had a Parisian *couturier* flown in at the last minute, all for the purpose of choosing the right tie for the right occasion, in such a way as to convey all that he felt for America and its system of democratic government. Jeremiah Greenfield, with one stroke of his word processor, had undone it all.

At a hastily called news conference, the president declared in the most solemn of tones, "I'll get to the bottom of this leak thing," pausing here for emphasis and dramatic effect, "if it's the only thing I ever do as president." There was common consensus that it probably would be.

C H A P T E R   7

July 2003

JEREMIAH CONTINUED TO TURN out his Washington stories. His
popularity continued to grow. Emma couldn't have been happier and decided it was time to celebrate. As a surprise for
Jeremiah, she made reservations for the two of them, Nick and
Janet – one of the many women in Nick's life – at a newly opened,
highly acclaimed restaurant in the Flatiron district. No one, including Emma, was happy in the elegant, over refined setting in which
every detail in the muted decor was chosen to harmonize with
every other, down to the color of the waitresses' uniforms. The
presentation of the food was striking. The wine list was impressive.
The cooking was satisfactory but unremarkable, the conversations
were subdued. Under such circumstances – with each of them feeling ill at ease for the same reason – the only thing to do was drink
too much, which is what the four of them did.

By the time they had finished their appetizers, they were unquestionably the loudest table in the restaurant. Several heads turned their way but the rowdy celebrants were oblivious.

"To Jeremiah Greenfield," said Nick, raising his glass, as dessert was meticulously placed on the table, "star Washington reporter."

"Yes," said Emma, chiming in, "to Jeremiah Greenfield, star Washington reporter, who fell on his ass and landed on his feet." The observation seemed to please no one so much as it did Emma, who laughed so hard she dropped her wineglass on the floor.

"To the woman of my life," said Jeremiah, raising his glass in Emma's direction, "whose charm and wit are exceeded only by the girth of her hips."

Jeremiah thought this was extremely funny and now he couldn't stop laughing.

"To Emma's hips," said Nick, raising his glass.

"There is nothing funny about my hips," said Emma, deadpan.

"There is nothing funny about my falling on my ass, assuming that in fact that is what I actually did," said Jeremiah, deadpan.

"I think your ass is just fine," said a proper-looking woman from the next table.

"Thank you," said Jeremiah, raising his glass in her direction.

"Jeremiah," said Nick, failing to raise his glass, "you are an ass, you know. That Washington drivel you turn out is a blight on mankind."

Janet gave Nick an elbow in the ribs.

"Let's get the check," said Jeremiah.

Emma and Janet went to the lady's room.

"That was nothing," said Nick. "I didn't mean it at all. I was just posturing. It's the fucking wine. That damned cabernet from California. I never liked it. It's junk. Gives me a headache. Only a dump like this would think of serving it," he said as the *maitre d'* arrived, inscrutable and solicitous, coats in hand, skillfully directing the errant diners towards the door.

The following morning Jeremiah woke up with a headache and a bad taste in his mouth.

He arrived at work on time, sat down at his desk and arranged his papers. There were three notebooks filled with information, tasty little tidbits with which to titillate his readers. All he had to do was pick one, dress it up, and give it a surprise twist at the end. He had done it many times before, but seemed unable to do it today. The words were not coming. None of his usual tricks was working. Something was in the way. He thought back to the night before. One phrase kept coming back. "A blight on mankind," Nick had said. Those words made Jeremiah nauseated with shame.

Jeremiah spent a week without coming up with a story. And then one afternoon after lunch, taking a leisurely walk back to the office, he got an idea. Maybe it was time for a change in strategy. He had proved himself at trivia. Maybe he should undertake something riskier. He let out the word that he was looking for new material. And in less than two weeks he found what he was looking for.

Apparently, a certain senator named Myron Brickbat had been offered a $50,000 bribe by Elliot Clearforest to vote for a bill that would have permitted logging interests to clear cut the states of California, Washington and Oregon. That such an offer should be tendered is certainly not surprising, nor is it newsworthy. That it should be refused, however, is astounding and unbelievable. And that's just what happened. And Anna Bandolla, who was sitting at her desk with tape recorder rolling, got it all for posterity.

"Here's the fifty thousand. Take it," said Elliot Clearforest, pushing a brown paper bag across the desk.

"No, I can't," said Myron Brickbat.

The next day this dialogue became known to an incredulous readership. From Bombay to Kalamazoo those three little words were on everyone's lips. "No, I can't." It got banner headlines in every major paper across the nation, and most minor ones. News and even weather reports were interrupted by excited reporters, "This just in. Washington senator turns down bribe."

What the public never learned was the rest of what Senator Brickbat had had to say in response to the offer of $50,000. The entire, unedited response, goes as follows:

"I can't accept it. I have ten safe deposit boxes stuffed full with greenbacks. I have sewed money into my mattress, my jock strap and the curtains in the den. I have buried it in the backyard, hidden it under floorboards in the attic, behind pictures in the wall and in Ziploc bags in our deep freezer. My wife says if I bring any more of the stuff into the house, I'm out and she's changing the locks."

The American people never heard the whole story. Instead they got a different one. For a brief moment there was a glimmer of hope that honesty and integrity might one day return to Washington. Brickbat and Clearforest became overnight celebrities. And of course, Jeremiah, the man who, with the invaluable assistance of Anna Bandolla, had made it all happen became associated in the nation's eyes with truth and virtue.

His picture appeared on the cover of *Time*, *Newsweek* and *People* magazines. He was interviewed on early-morning, mid-afternoon and late-night talk shows. A television sitcom, featuring an investigative reporter working "for a small newspaper somewhere in suburban New Jersey," became an immediate success. Schools of journalism were flooded with applications. The president, despite his distrust and bitter hatred for Jeremiah, personally, over a nationwide satellite hook-up, invited Jeremiah to a gala, black tie dinner at the White House at which he, himself, ate crow. From the first toast and forkful of pâté, to the final passing of wind, the nation, rapt with attention, followed the event in the next day's papers. Of course, no one actually believed the story as written. But they wanted to, and so they did, just as they believed in their counterfeit marriages, boring jobs and religions of choice.

CHAPTER 8

August 2003

Shortly after Jeremiah's "Clearforest" story broke, Nick was on his way home after a routine day at work. He was approached by a well-dressed, well-spoken, slick, wavy-haired Anglo-Saxon who identified himself as Bob. Bob asked Nick to join him for a beer at one of the local pubs, explaining that he had an interesting proposition for Nick to consider. Nick thought that perhaps Bob was a pimp for the local head hunter or maybe someone with encyclopedias to sell. He decided to take his chances and accepted Bob's offer of a beer.

"We all want the same thing for America," Bob began, once the two men had found themselves a comfortable spot in O'Leary's Twenty-Four Hour All Irish Pub. "We want her to remain the great nation we know she can be."

Nick stared blankly into Bob's blank slab of a face, periodically returning to his beer.

"As you and I both know, this country has seen some hard times," Bob continued, tracing the decline of the American presidency from FDR to the resignation of Richard Milhouse Nixon, offering especial reverence for Calvin Coolidge and Herbert Hoover, "two of the greatest men America has ever known."

"It was as a consequence of the Watergate hearings – which have done more than any occurrence in the history of the republic to tarnish America's image in the world and undermine her belief in herself – that a group of us got together to discuss what could be done to restore America's belief in her Godhead, the manifestation of all that is noble and manly, the American president. It matters little to me," he said, sitting up in his seat, staring straight at Nick with eyes of Carborundum, momentarily shedding his veneer of affability, "who is in the White House or which party put him there. What matters is that the myth of the presidency continues undisturbed as an icon before which Americans bow. Because if this icon is destroyed, Mr. Belladonna, we will all of us perish in the rubble." Bob paused, took the red silk handkerchief out of his breast pocket, wiped beads of perspiration off his brow and then continued in a more conversational manner.

"The American presidency has nothing to do with balance of power, budget making, diplomacy or the price of sugar. It has one very simple purpose, a purpose so obvious that it could easily escape notice, yet so fundamental that should this purpose not be fulfilled, the foundations of world civilization would be permanently destroyed."

Here he started becoming intense again.

"When men and women, young and old, little girls and little boys get out of bed in the morning, they do so with an assumption which constitutes the basis for their psychological existence. They do so with the understanding that a man is in charge," he said, letting both hands fall to the table for emphasis. "And that, Mr. Belladonna, is what the presidency is all about." Then Bob stopped, gave a short nervous laugh, wiped the corner of his mouth and reassured Nick, with a relaxed smile, that the worst was over.

This, Bob explained, was why he and his friends had formed CRAP (Committee to Resurrect the American Presidency), to ensure that manliness prevailed in our culture and hence throughout the world, making snide reference to Great Britain, "a nation of faggots, where women were allowed to rule and look at what has happened to them."

"We can't do this important work alone, Mr. Belladonna. We need men like you to help us. I know you are friends with Jeremiah Greenfield. It has been brought to our attention that he has this silly hobby of making an imaginary run for the presidency. Now that he is a national figure, his hobby is beginning to worry us. It's probably perfectly harmless, but one can't be too careful. Sometimes innocent gestures like this undermine the seriousness of purpose surrounding the presidency and give people ideas that we don't want them to have. We are prepared to pay you handsomely if you are willing to bring us up to date every so often about his activities." At this, Bob opened up the attaché case he had brought in with him. It was filled with stacks of twenties. "And that's just the beginning," he said.

Nick looked but said nothing. He was wondering how Bob had found out about Jeremiah's presidential ambitions. Bob took his unresponsiveness for hesitancy and actually upped the ante. Nick accepted the offer, quickly banishing from his mind any thought that there was something unsavory about such dealings or that he might be betraying his close friend.

Several weeks passed and Bob reappeared. A routine was established. Over beer at O'Leary's, Bob would enlighten Nick on the inherent vileness of females of all species, inveigh against a particular woman writer who might have just published a book, some defender of abortion rights – "just another plot to free themselves from the yoke of motherhood" – and a man or two who might have adopted the woman's cause. For them he had even greater contempt than for women themselves. During these conversations Bob would ask some casual questions about Jeremiah and Nick would answer him honestly, since there was nothing to hide. He would pass along the latest version of a poster, or a campaign button, or a speech Jeremiah had written, some of which Bob found quite impressive.

"Has Jeremiah given any indication that he might actually be planning to run in '04?" Bob asked during one of their meetings. "Has he been approached by any backers? Has he approached any himself?"

"No. Not that I know of. But what would be so terrible if Jeremiah became president? He is male, after all."

"Let's just say he is not one of us," said Bob, with a raise of his eyebrows and a knowing look.

That was good enough for Nick.

CHAPTER 9

Two Weeks Later

A FEW WEEKS AFTER NICK'S first meeting with Bob, he was sitting across from Jeremiah at Jeremiah's desk, planning a shoot for a story they were working on together. In walked a short, energetic fellow dressed in a Nantucket red sports jacket and an iridescent tie, identifying himself as Maximilian Popoff. Max worked for a public relations firm that organized "electoral congresses," as he liked to refer to them. He wanted to speak in private with Jeremiah. Jeremiah explained that anyone who wanted to speak with him wanted to speak with his good friend Nick Belladonna. That was just fine with Popoff.

In the friendliest of tones Max explained to Jeremiah that there would be a special kind of meeting to which he was an invited guest.

"Jeremiah," he asked in a conversational way, "have you ever gone to summer camp?"

"No," answered Jeremiah.

"Well, all right, let's just make believe you have. Though it's really not critical. Nowadays camp directors get together as a group and sponsor what are called 'camp fairs.' These are occasions for parents to learn something about the different camps available for their children. It's a chance for directors to make themselves known and see what's out there.

"Another example might be representatives of various businesses and public agencies setting up tables on a college campus. It's an opportunity to make some matches between employers and prospective employees. Are you with me?"

"I'm not so sure," said Jeremiah, toying with the telephone cord.

"Hold on," said Max, "we're getting there. The presidency is run just like one of the college recruiting events or a camp fair. Representatives from various interest groups get together at one location for the purposes of sizing up the candidates. Potential candidates are given an opportunity to display their wares, so to speak. Ultimately, alliances are formed and various coalitions unite behind one favored personality. This kind of event has replaced what used to be derisively referred to as 'smoke filled rooms.' Times have changed Jeremiah. There's no smoking at all. Are you with me?"

"I think so," said Jeremiah.

"Bear in mind that the initial pool of candidates is relatively large, as many as thirty or more. At the outset, the attrition rate is high. After a lot of bargaining, a select group of candidates is ready for presentation to the public. Some, as visible as yourself, with a strong public image, should do well. Can we count on you being there? It's a week from Monday. This could be a big opportunity for you."

Jeremiah gave a look Nick's way. Nick gave an imperceptible nod.

"Sure, I'll be there," said Jeremiah.

"Great. Nick is invited, too. See you then. It's at the Hilton. It starts at nine in the morning. Take the elevator to the third floor and there will be someone waiting for you."

"Oh, one thing," said Max before ending the conversation, "it

41

would be better if you didn't tell anyone about this. No one. Not even your wife."

"Can you believe it?" asked Jeremiah, once Popoff was out of ear shot. "All these years of planning and waiting and then *poof*," he puffed out his cheeks and made a gesture with his hand, as if setting a fragile piece of glassware on the shelf, "there it is."

"Rent yourself a tux and be prepared to make a little speech," Nick advised Jeremiah.

One Monday passed and the next one arrived. Just as Popoff said, there was an attractive, long-legged woman waiting to greet Jeremiah and Nick as they got out of the elevator on the third floor of the Hilton.

"You're Mr. Greenfield, aren't you? And you're Mr. Belladonna. I'm Mary Ann," she said pleasantly, as she extended her hand to each of them in turn. "Follow me."

Jeremiah and Nick were led down a long corridor and into a small room which was almost empty except for a table and three chairs which were flush against the wall.

"Why don't you sit down over there," said their hostess, as she reached under the table.

There was a click and the table and chairs, the wall and a semi-circular piece of the floor began rotating. When the rotation was complete, Jeremiah and Nick found themselves on a stage in a very large meeting room filled with people, tables and booths. A bell was sounded and the noise subsided. The hostess rose from her seat, took a microphone and in the clearest of tones announced, "This is Jeremiah Greenfield."

There was a round of applause.

Mary Ann signaled and Jeremiah rose.

"Why don't you take a walk down that apron so the folks can get a better look at you," said Mary Ann.

Jeremiah walked down the apron, stood looking out into the crowd, his head held high, a smile on his face.

There was another round of applause.

"Why don't you say a few words," said Mary Ann, extending the microphone in his direction.

Jeremiah made his way back down the apron and took the microphone.

"I am pleased to be here," he said in relaxed tones, making it up as he went along. "I am honored to have been chosen to participate in this gathering which is proof, if ever we needed it, that democracy is alive and well in this great country of ours."

Applause.

"I can remember when I was a youngster visiting Washington – I couldn't have been more than five – my grandfather took me by the hand and walked me up to the gates of the White House. Pointing with pride he said, 'Therein has lived many a rogue and a villain.'"

"Those are words I have never forgotten," said Jeremiah. "It is my fondest hope, that one day, with your help," he said, gesturing to the audience, "I can continue on in that tradition and dish up a plate of lies unlike anything this nation has ever seen."

To applause and cheering, Jeremiah handed the microphone back to Mary Ann who led him off the stage and on to the convention floor.

Jeremiah was greeted by many well-wishers, each of whom tried to sweet talk him into the direction of his booth or table. There must have been close to forty installations in all, lined up in aisles as one might see at the "Motorboat Show" or at a street fair on Columbus Avenue, each with its banners, placards, posters, and buttons advocating its particular point of view, each with hospitality suites scattered throughout the hotel where representatives met in seclusion with individual candidates, treated them to gourmet snacks, buffets and sometimes full meals, passed along gold-plated paper weights, coffee mugs and sometimes freshly printed hundred dollar bills, just as a tease.

There were representatives of the nuclear and oil industries, the prison-industrial-complex, and bio-genetic-agri-business. There were booths for defense contractors, road builders and pharmaceuticals; there was a booth representing the "Coalition for Freedom and Justice," a small renegade group of former CIA agents; there were industrialists, solid conservatives with a focus on a stable domestic economy, high unemployment and cheap labor, led by a man named Cawley Watson; there was a consortium of speculative bankers, brokers and lawyers whose focus was on huge profits over the short run and an unstable economy; there were tables for doctors, lawyers, labor and utilities; there were representatives from foreign countries, each with a special interest in the outcome of the next election.

Then there were the candidates themselves – all male, all white, former actors, athletes, rock stars – moving from table to table, shaking hands, giving their views carefully tailored to reflect the interests of the particular representative they were speaking to.

It was a lively event. There were announcements and a fair amount of speechifying over the span of this three-day convention, just about every special interest given the opportunity to advocate its particular viewpoint.

Jeremiah was well-received and invited to follow-up sessions with various interest groups. He was on his way.

CHAPTER 10

Early September 2003

NICK SPENT A FAIR amount of time over at Jeremiah's, more so than usual, now that Jeremiah had become politically visible and Nick was on wavy-haired Bob's payroll. Jeremiah was flattered by the attention. Emma was bothered, and didn't hide it. Nick helped himself liberally to his friend's supply of Scotch whiskey. Emma threatened to charge him by the glass. And meant it.

The three had just finished a game of pinochle and were all watching the eleven o'clock news – Emma had just taken a spoonful of Ben and Jerry's low fat, mocha latte ice cream – when Jeremiah became visibly disturbed.

"A particularly homely looking secretary was found floating down the Potomac River this morning," said the striking, light-skinned black woman, placing the time of death several weeks earlier, which would have made it shortly after the "Clearforest-

Brickbat" story. She then went on to describe the secretary's bulging eyes and the panty hose wrapped around her neck. Then a photograph flashed on the screen of Anna Bandolla, with a gap-toothed smile on her pockmarked face, and her arm around none other than Jeremiah Greenfield. Jeremiah's jaw dropped. Emma looked at Nick. Nick looked at Jeremiah. No one knew what to say.

The following morning, Jeremiah was in Nick's office. Maynard appeared.

"Was that you I saw on TV last night with your arm around a particularly homely and now dead secretary?"

"Yes, it was," said Jeremiah, trying to figure out what Maynard might be thinking, determined not to reveal the true meaning of the photograph.

"I can't say I admire your choice in women. How did you know her?"

"She was a cousin of mine, on my sister's side of the family."

"I am not so sure," continued Maynard, leaning against the edge of the desk, "how this will affect your following."

A few days later, Jeremiah received a call at home. The caller identified himself only as Sal and said he had an interesting story for Jeremiah to consider.

"Okay," said Jeremiah, "I'll be right over."

"Where are you going?" asked Emma.

"I've got an important lead," said Jeremiah. "I'll be back in about an hour."

"Be careful, *liebling*," she said.

Bigaldi's is one of those many *pasticcerias* in the West Village that sell mediocre pastry with much flourish and pride to an admiring public from the south shore of Long Island, where this is as good as it gets.

Two men were sitting at the *cappuccino* bar talking loudly and laughing. When Jeremiah came in, one of them turned around and said hello.

"Jeremiah," he said. "How's it goin'?"

He was big. Big-fisted. About six-two, 250 pounds. Large neck. Broad chest. Buttons on his sports jacket popping.

"Over here," he said, in a most friendly, gregarious manner, pointing to a table in the back.

"What'll it be?" he asked. "The *cannoli* you gotta try. Hey *amico*," he yelled, "some *cannoli* for my friend here."

"So you're Sal," Jeremiah said, trying to get things on track.

"No," he said. "Sal couldn't make it. I'm Bruno. Try one of the *cannoli*," he insisted. "You're gonna love 'em."

Jeremiah took a bite. The filling had the consistency and taste of wallpaper paste.

"Terrific," he said.

"Jerry, do you mind if I call you Jerry?" asked Bruno, biting into a *cannoli*. "You know you make a lot of people unhappy with your Brickbat story. A lot of people. I know it's not what you meant. But that's the way it happened. My philosophy is, 'What's private is private. Business is business.' Sometimes the wheels need a little grease. Sometimes they don't. Everybody knows that and nobody cares. It's not what people want to read about in the morning paper. Earthquakes, typhoons, murder, rape, robbery. This is what your readers want. Take my word for it. They love it. Can't get enough of it. I myself could spend half the morning reading about one good earthquake. It's in the details. You know that. It's fascinating stuff. Listen," said Bruno, reaching into his breast pocket and coming out with an envelope, "could be you've been working too hard. It happens to all of us. Everyone could use some rest. Give you the time to come up with some new ideas. You'll love this place. It's off the coast at Fort Meyers. Beautiful beach. Beautiful ocean. Here's the ticket. Everything first class. Oh, I almost forgot. Do you cook? I'm a good cook. In two weeks I'm having some people over, actors, directors, producers, the mayor, the governor, the cardinal, everybody will be there. You're gonna come. Here," he said, writing an address in the west 50s on a napkin. "Don't forget," he said, clapping Jeremiah across the shoulder in a gesture of friendship, signaling an end to the encounter.

Bruno got up from the table. Jeremiah didn't move. He looked at the envelope and tried to make sense out of what had just happened. For some reason he couldn't help liking Bruno. Maybe he had come along at the right moment. Maybe Jeremiah had lost track of who he was and where he was headed. This would be an opportunity to rethink things and set a new course.

He was thus reasoning with himself when he felt a cold, hard cylindrical object pressed up against his left temple. His breathing stopped. Every muscle in his body contracted. He started counting in his head as if he were playing a game of hide and seek – one Mississippi, two Mississippi – waiting for the gun to go off. He had just completed three Mississippi and was on his way to four.

"We can count on you, can't we, Jerry?" said Bruno as he pulled the gun away.

Jeremiah had a burning urge to urinate but didn't want to move. He picked up a *cannoli* with the intention of biting into it. His hand was trembling. The *cannoli* fell onto the plate.

Jeremiah rested his hands on the table, palms down, and focused on breathing. Where would he find the courage to walk out the door past Bruno and his friends?

There was a bathroom straight in front of him. The exit was in the opposite direction. He got up from the table and headed straight for the bathroom. He relieved his bladder, threw cold water on his face and looked at himself in the mirror. What he saw he didn't like. He was looking into the eyes of a frightened little boy, desperate for attention and acceptance.

He braced himself against the edge of the sink. He wanted to weep but would not let himself. Then suddenly he slammed his fist into the side of the sink.

"No way," he roared. "No goddamn fucking way."

He took the envelope out of his pocket and strode up to where Bruno was seated.

"Thanks, but no thanks," he said, dropping the envelope on the counter.

Jeremiah walked out of the shop and took a slow, long walk

48

home, kicking a few garbage cans along the way. His fear had turned to rage. By the time he was half way home his rage had turned to confusion and then self-doubt.

Hadn't he been feeding his readers the mixture of sentimentality and irrelevancy they craved and didn't they love him for it? This one time he had dug down a little deeper and come up with something more controversial. But isn't it common knowledge that senators are bribed? And if it is, why did someone just put a gun to his head?

Jeremiah was up against the reality one, reality two problem, but he didn't know it. Reality one is the image of politics that is hand-tailored to meet the expectations of the viewing public. Reality two is the version that takes place behind closed doors. To allow reality two to intrude upon reality one is like adding phosphorous to water. There will be an explosion.

The following morning Jeremiah was at work organizing his papers. He noticed an envelope with his name on it in the one clear space on his desk near the telephone. He casually picked it up and opened it. The tickets to Fort Meyers that he had returned to Bruno the night before. His skin turned cold. His hand trembled slightly as he held the envelope. It took but a moment's reflection to realize that he would be taking a trip to Florida. He explained to Maynard that he would be out of town for a long weekend. Emma seemed pleased and asked no questions.

At 10:00 A.M. the next day, Jeremiah was on a plane to Fort Meyers. During the flight he struck up a conversation with a German couple who were staying at the same resort. They rented a car and drove him to the hotel.

The island was even more beautiful than Bruno had said. A wide strip of fine, white sand stretched out into the distance along the emerald-colored sea. Jeremiah rose early the following morning and took a run by the water. He ate a sumptuous breakfast and settled into a book he had brought along entitled, *The Politics of Lying*. He rented a sailboat after lunch and got a little too much sun. He had a dinner of fresh fish on a terrace overlooking the surf.

The next morning he awoke and felt lethargic and empty. He realized two things. One, he was no longer completely in charge of his own existence. He was sharing the power with an unknown, hidden force. Two, he had attained notoriety as a journalist trading in half-truths, lies and triviality, and in the process had gotten lost. Who was he and where was he headed? The more he pondered these questions, the more despondent he became. Three days ago a gun had been put to his head. Standing in the bathroom, looking into the mirror, he had seen who he really was. Would he have the courage to face up to what he had seen?

For the first time in his life Jeremiah had the sense that there was a larger world that contained him. He was beginning to understand that his actions had a consequence and that that consequence, like a boomerang, could come right back at him from behind and catch him in the neck. It had always seemed to him that he could sail off in any direction without hindrance if only he could determine his destination. Now Jeremiah could see that the harbor was patrolled and that he had to get past Bruno to reach open sea.

Upon his return, Jeremiah tried to keep things going at the *Ledger* as if nothing had changed. Maynard could see that something had gone wrong but said nothing. The excitement of success had faded for Jeremiah. Too much had happened for him simply to proceed with business as usual. He was unsettled and anxious. Recent events had triggered the Allworth response. He was back on that stage licking up vomit.

His Washington trivia were nothing but lies, irrelevant fragments of information taken out of context and offered as a substitute for the real truth, the whole truth. The Brickbat story was a lie, too, which is to say, only half the truth. Sure a senator had turned down a bribe. And yes, that is newsworthy. However, what would his readers have thought if they knew the real reason that the bribe was turned down? Hadn't he deliberately misled and betrayed them?

"A panderer, that's what I am," Jeremiah said to Nick one day over lunch, "selling out to the basest instincts in a corrupt and immoral society. A whore and a pimp all in one, crawling on my belly in the muck and mire of life."

He had had enough of that, he said, and was going to tell Maynard.

Instead of his usual slump, Jeremiah actually stood up straight.

"Maynard," he said, "my heart's not in it."

"Nah, you've had too much vacation," Maynard said, making a veiled reference to Jeremiah's unexplained trip to Florida. Maynard leaned forward with his elbows on the desk, sliding into the word "vacation" with sarcastic emphasis. "You'll be back into the swing of things in no time flat."

"Maybe I don't want to 'be back into the swing of things,'" Jeremiah said, now looking straight at Maynard and echoing his sarcasm.

"Jeremiah, what's happened to you? Don't be a fool. You're as greedy and as corrupt as the rest of us. Don't try and set yourself apart. There is no money in it."

"I don't care about money," said Jeremiah moodily.

Maynard knew this was true. Jeremiah had done it all for the recognition and it seemed as if now he didn't even care about that. Maynard was getting desperate. He felt he was losing his hold on Jeremiah.

"Jeremiah," he said, "just tell me what you want. Whatever it is. Just tell me."

"I'm going for a walk," he said, leaving Maynard standing in the doorway to his office, his black skin the color of ivory.

Nick followed Jeremiah out of the building into the glaring sunlight. They crossed the street to Hard Times Square and found themselves a bench in the shade. Jeremiah picked up where he had left off with Maynard.

"I've lost my identity and sense of purpose," he said. "I've lost my reason for getting up in the morning. I've even lost my appetite."

The more he thought about his life, the worse he felt. Questioning everything he had taken for granted, he sank deeper and deeper into a Cartesian stupor. Being what he didn't want to be and could no longer tolerate being, but not having fully resigned himself to nothingness, he was sliding off a cliff of meaning into a cesspool of decay which he had devoted his life to escaping. After what seemed like a journey without end, Jeremiah reached bottom, not with a crash, but with the slide of an elevator as it slips into position before the door opens. He had fallen deep and was surrounded by darkness, but at least he had stopped falling.

Then a voice broke the quiet, a raspy, irritating voice. It was the voice of a tall, thin, scantily clad black man who was pushing a shopping cart filled with the detritus of middle-class civilization. There was an old clock radio, a hair dryer, a couple of pillows, some empty soda cans and, in the front, propped up in the seat that would have been for a child, was a stuffed Snoopy to which he was singing, "Hang on, Snoopy, hang on," periodically taking a sip from a bottle of natural spring water and then sharing some with Snoopy.

"Yo, bro, why so low?" the black man asked his Snoopy.

"You talking to me?" asked Jeremiah in a tired voice.

"Jeremiah," said Nick, "I don't think he is interested in your tale of woe."

"How do you know?" asked Jeremiah.

"What makes you think I'm low?" said Jeremiah, returning to the black man, intrigued by the possibility of penetrating the nether world of homelessness, feeling lower even than this lowly creature and hoping that this hopeless wretch would open his arms to him.

"Yo, bro, why so low?" the black man repeated again to his Snoopy, in a ritualistic way, showing more interest in this stuffed animal than in Jeremiah. Jeremiah got up and started walking towards the black man, talking as he walked, as if the black man were a dog who had gotten off his leash, whom Jeremiah had to soothingly distract until he could get the leash back around his neck.

"You live here, friend?" asked Jeremiah. "I work over der," he said, trying to talk black.

"Git," said the black man, almost hissing at Jeremiah, holding his Snoopy in front of him as if it were a cross and Jeremiah were a vampire. "Git, you fuckin' honky shit."

Jeremiah took this as a friendly overture by a man who was beat down and suspicious.

"Say, bro, I ain't gonna do you no harm, motha fuckah," said Jeremiah, like someone doing bird calls for the first time.

"Don't give me that fuckin shit, man."

Jeremiah took a handkerchief out of his pocket and fashioned it in the shape of a rabbit's head.

"Yo, bro. Go slo," said Jeremiah, talking to his handkerchief.

This got the black man's attention.

"I'm broke. No joke," said Jeremiah. "Broke down inside. No place to hide. Lost the race. Falling on my face."

"Don't be a schmo, Joe. Go with the flow," said homeless man to his Snoopy.

"Going with the flow." Now there was an idea. That's what Jeremiah thought he had been doing all along. But of course he hadn't been. He had been too busy working off the blueprint that his father had handed down to him as an antidote to his own failure.

"Make something of yourself. Don't be a bum like me," his father had once said to him.

So that was it. That's what was in his way. He had sold his soul over a tattered blueprint and a worthless father. But what was he to do now that he had figured it all out?

"'Go with the flow,' that's what it's all about," said Jeremiah to Nick with a foolish-looking grin on his face.

Nick didn't have the heart to disagree.

CHAPTER 11

That Evening

BY THE TIME NICK and Jeremiah got back to the office, the place was empty. Nick began collecting his things for the trip home. Jeremiah was gazing out into the setting sun across Hard Times Square, perhaps waiting for something to flow through him, as homeless man had suggested. Should he continue with the *Ledger*, maybe going back to covering funerals and social events and forgetting about Washington altogether? Should he quit his job and try something completely different? Any and all possibilities lay before him.

Nick did nothing to dissuade Jeremiah from any of the suggestions he threw out, debated with him the pros and cons as would any neutral participant, all the time deliberately, subtly trying to tilt the argument in favor of the status quo. For as long as Jeremiah was in the public eye, he was a potential candidate for president and Mr.

Bob would be paying Nick his periodic visits with a bag full of twenties. It was as if Nick were in a struggle with homeless man over Jeremiah's soul — Nick the Devil and homeless man the Archangel — and Nick was losing.

"Go with the flow," Jeremiah would repeat. "I wonder what he meant by it. Do you think he meant?..."

"Jeremiah," said Nick, "it's time to go."

Nick, never one to turn down a free meal, accepted Jeremiah's invitation to come home with him for dinner. Jeremiah wanted Nick to be there as a witness for what had happened in Hard Times Square and help convince Emma of the importance of what he had learned. He went home drooling with flow, eager to tell Emma everything about his important discovery, explore with her life's possibilities.

"You been in the sun too long?" she snapped at him, pushing past him as she walked into the kitchen. Of course poor Emma had no way of knowing that this was a new Jeremiah who wasn't to be pushed around.

"That was a mistake," he said coolly.

"*Liebling*, I'm sorry," said Emma, like a prize fighter reeling from a punch that she hadn't seen coming, looking for an opening of her own. "Tell me more about your talk with the man in the square. It sounds interesting."

"Get me some grub," he said gruffly, subconsciously aping some of the tough talk from the grade B westerns he watched on television.

"*Liebling*," Emma yelled from the kitchen, "be a good boy and set the table."

Jeremiah didn't move. Emma paused in the doorway to the living room, looking at her husband as he sat in his undershirt, with a can of beer in his hand, aware that either she was seeing him for the first time or that something dramatic had happened to change his character and personality. The only thing she could think of was that there was someone else. It's the first thing any woman would think of under such circumstances and under these circumstances, Emma was just another woman.

She paid careful attention to the meal she was preparing and added some special touches that she knew Jeremiah would like – garlic bread and Alka Seltzer – and for herself some Ben and Jerry's Chocolate Chip Cookie Dough ice cream. She chilled a bottle of white wine and lit some candles, ignoring Nick's presence as best she could.

Emma spoke to Jeremiah in the gentlest of tones about nothing in particular, the soap operas she had watched that day, her conversations with Marge, who was having a hysterectomy; Gloria, who was having a face-lift; and Loretta, whose tubes were being tied. Jeremiah feigned indifference and kept interrupting her with irrelevant tidbits directed at Nick, using him as a foil to get at Emma.

"How was your trip?" Emma asked innocently.

"My trip?" he mused, not sure what she was talking about. "Oh, my trip. That was fine. Just fine."

"Where did you go?" she asked.

"Where did I go?" he repeated, not fully hearing what either one of them was saying. "Where did I go? Well, I went to India and Pakistan. I went to Tucson and Sante Fe and then I went to the dogs. I'm not sure I'm back yet."

This was not the kind of information Emma was looking for.

"Did you meet anyone interesting?"

"Meet anyone interesting?" he repeated. "Well, I don't know. I suppose so. Maybe."

Then she stopped beating about the bush.

"Jeremiah, you seem strange, different. Is there someone else?"

"What do you mean?" he asked, confused.

"You know. Is there someone else?" she persisted, picking at a piece of sausage with her fork.

"I don't know what the hell you're talking about and if I did, it's none of your damned business anyway," he said. "Pass me some bread."

Emma passed the bread and glared at her husband.

Jeremiah rested his fork on his plate and returned her glare.

Nick cleared his throat nervously.

"What about Anna?" asked Emma.

"What do you mean? Who are you talking about?"

"The one you were on television with, the one with the gap-tooth smile who had her arm around you. That one. You were in love with her, weren't you?" asked Emma, holding the butter knife on the table as if it were a dagger.

"You're out of your mind," said Jeremiah, surprised to see Emma expressing jealousy. "And suppose I did love her, why should it matter to you? You're too damned busy with your soap operas, your girlfriends and your mother to notice who I am or where I am."

"And why should I? A worthless heap of trash, that's all you are. But if I ever find out you're with another woman, I'll shoot your balls off."

CHAPTER 12

THE NEXT MORNING, NICK found Jeremiah seated at his desk, idly stirring his coffee with his index finger.

"The truth. That's what homeless man had meant without saying it," said Jeremiah, before Nick even had a chance to sit down. "'Go with the truth, Ruth.' That was the hidden message."

Nick sat down but did not respond.

Maynard appeared. Nick had left him some photos. A Mafioso shot dead while relieving his bowel. A heavy-set man in his sixties, pants at his ankles, shirt discreetly covering his genitals, head hanging back, eyes wide open in disbelief, arms hanging limply at his sides, body sagging into the upturned lid of the toilet, clearly unprepared for what had befallen him. Every caution he must have taken, taken in vain. Dead by any measure.

"Memorial services over in Jersey City. One bullet between the eyes, while he was taking a crap. We got some great photos. Here,"

Maynard said, throwing the photos on Jeremiah's desk. "The address is on the back of one of them."

Jeremiah casually picked up one of the photos.

"I don't do funerals," said Jeremiah to himself, but loud enough so Maynard could hear. That brought Maynard back.

"What did you say?" he asked.

"I said I don't do funerals."

"Just what do you do?" asked Maynard.

"I haven't decided yet," said Jeremiah.

"When you do decide, kindly let me know," said Maynard. "You've got till Friday."

Under the circumstances, Jeremiah should have been worried, but he wasn't. He could always do something. Or then again, he might choose to do nothing. That was a thought. There was his homeless friend in Hard Times Square with his Snoopy and a shopping cart full of junk, staying alive and working at it in his way. Jeremiah could always join him.

Four o'clock rolled around and Jeremiah had not done a stitch of work all day.

"Jeremiah," Nick said, carefully choosing his words, "I think Maynard means business."

"Don't be a schmo, Joe. Go with the flow."

"Jeremiah," Nick said, starting to get a little bothered, "that guy in the square is a bum. His brain is rotted out from cheap booze. He doesn't know what he is talking about. He is lost. He doesn't even know the day of the week."

No, Jeremiah persisted, homeless man – whom Jeremiah now was beginning to portray as Mercury in bum's clothing – was trying to tell him something very important.

"Well, maybe he has read you," said Nick, warming to his subject and momentarily dropping his facade of calculated neutrality. "Maybe he has seen through the superficiality, the worship of fame, the acquiescence to the very middle-class values you claim to scorn, to the depths of your cravenly being."

"Who the hell are you to pass judgment?" said Jeremiah, slamming the desk drawer shut.

"Jeremiah," said Nick coolly, "spare me your misty-eyed visions of the truth. We are living in a corrupt society. We have all been bought and sold many times over. No one wants the truth. Least of all you."

"It is not a 'misty-eyed vision,'" replied Jeremiah. "It's what we see when we take away the lie. Every half-truth and apology, illusion and self-deception, exposed for what it is."

"You want the truth?" said Nick. "The truth is you are married to a cow and you're miserable. *That* is the truth," said Nick triumphantly.

Jeremiah gritted his teeth.

"That's not true," he said, rising from his chair and walking over to the window.

Nick sensed that Jeremiah was wavering.

"Jeremiah," he said, two horns sprouting out of the middle of his head, "everyone is fascinated with the lie, not just you. The man in the front row knows he is being lied to, but is delighted at having had one put over on him, at seeing the rabbit pulled out of the hat yet another time, all at once experiencing the double nature of reality, the lie and the truth, without ever having to come to terms with either."

Jeremiah's eyes were riveted on Nick's. Now he could see how totally ludicrous it had been for him or anyone to ever be serious about the truth in a practical way, and how to claim to be was a lie, perhaps the biggest and best lie of all. The message he had been given by Destiny was just another deception designed to make him feel small and impotent. The lie, his lie, everyone's lie, the middle-class lie, all of these lies taken together were the truth and essence of life. They gave life its meaning, made it work and cohere. Life without the lie was chaos. How foolish of him to have thought otherwise for even a minute. Nick could feel an irrepressible smile working its way from one corner of his mouth to the other.

Confused and distracted by the compelling alternatives he saw before him, Jeremiah pulled out the bottom drawer of his desk and found a resting place for his feet. Folding his hands across his lap, he closed his eyes and soon he was breathing heavily.

Nick sat there watching Jeremiah as he slept. At such a moment Jeremiah seemed like a lost child – Nick's child. It was Nick's job to take care of and protect him. And what was he doing? Taking advantage of this innocent creature. What would Jeremiah think if he ever found out?

"Jeremiah," said Nick, shaking his shoulder a little, "it's getting late."

Jeremiah opened his eyes and in a quiet, distant voice started talking before he was even fully awake.

"I had a dream," he said. "I was standing alone and naked on an open plain with an enormous erection, an erection that stretched out for miles and miles, up into the clouds and out of sight, an erection so wide and strong that it supported a three-lane highway, one lane in each direction and a middle lane for passing. At the end of this erection, somewhere hidden in the distance and out of sight, was the answer to life's meaning. I began pulling in this enormous penis of mine so I could see what was at the end, and as I pulled I could see the highway disappearing inside me, a highway lined with trees and grass for miles. Then came the used car lots and fast food centers, the cities and suburbs, hot dog and fruit stands, rest stops, magnificent views into the valley below and the mountains beyond, all passing before me as I pulled in this enormous erection so I could see what was at the end. As I was pulling, the erection changed to a fishing pole and I was turning the reel and pulling in faces from the river, smiling faces that I looked at and then shook off and threw back, faces of Emma, my mother, my father, other faces from the past that I no longer recognized. Then I pulled and the line wouldn't give. I had hooked something big. I pulled and pulled against the heavy weight and was dragged into the water as I tried to find what was at the end of the line. Then I hit bottom. It looked like Hard Times Square but was filled with beautifully colored fish. I felt someone tapping on my shoulder. I turned to look. It was homeless man, who then disappeared as I woke up."

"Jeremiah," said Nick, this time with more compassion than disgust, "it's time to go."

Nick led Jeremiah down the steps and out onto the street. Jeremiah squinted into the light of the ending day and then sneezed a powerful sneeze which brought him to his senses. In a flash he saw it all. What was it that Emma had been saying for years? "*Liebling*, some day you'll be a man." That's what his dream was telling him: "Be a man."

"And what do men do, Nick, real men, men with hair on their chests? They fuck. They fuck hard and often and long. And in that fucking, they bring the life process to its fullest expression and ultimate meaning, a meaning which defies logic, both Euclidean and non-Euclidean, meaning which goes beyond the Heisenberg uncertainty principle, the Peter principle and the principle of honor among thieves. The everlasting lay, therein lies the hidden meaning of life," said Jeremiah, his eyes wide with amazement. "That's it. Don't you see it, Nick?"

"Yeah," said Nick. "I'm beginning to see it."-

CHAPTER 13

The End of the Week

FRIDAY CAME AND FOUND Jeremiah where he had been all week, floating on his back, adrift in a sea of indecision. The morning was overcast. As Nick and Jeremiah walked past Hard Times Square, they could see homeless man through the shadows and fog on the other side of the fountain, curled up on a bench, covered with cardboard, holding his Snoopy, his shopping cart parked alongside, perfectly content by all outward appearances.

"How long can a person go on living like that?" asked Jeremiah, "assuming he doesn't get killed by a random bullet or some drifter who does it out of pure meanness? What does he do for his birthday? Does he even know when it is? So solitary, so painfully solitary..."

Homeless man looked content. Jeremiah was the lonely one, disconnected from the reality he was living, cursed with the ability to

see past the illusion to the ineffable emptiness of middle-class existence. All of this stone sober. To live with the illusion and to know
that he was living it as he lived it, this Jeremiah was finding impossible, as any shyster lawyer, demagogue, preacher or philosopher
could have told him in the first place. And so sat Cassandra
Greenfield, an example of someone who has seen the truth and
can't come back, which is why more money is spent protecting the
lie than even building bombs and bullets.

The fog was beginning to lift over Hard Times Square. Homeless
man was stirring on the bench. Carefully he removed the cardboard and, holding his Snoopy to his chest, where Snoopy had been
all night long, he rose to a sitting position and rubbed his eyes.

"There is the reality behind the illusion," Nick said to Jeremiah as
they watched homeless man go through his morning routine, folding up his carton, washing himself in the fountain, washing Snoopy's
hands and face with a piece of shredded cloth. Then, miracle of mir-
acles, he took out a toothbrush that he kept neatly and cleanly in its
original plastic container and began brushing his teeth. No toothpaste, though. No Aim, Crest, Best or Zest to squeeze from a tube,
the way middle-class man does, squeezing the nectar from life,
brushing it across his teeth and then spitting it out into the sink.
No, homeless man had no toothpaste and it was that more than anything else which separated him from his middle-class brothers and
sisters. Man reduced to his primeval truth. Man without his toothpaste. That was what homelessness was about.

By the time Nick and Jeremiah made it to the office it was ten
o'clock. Maynard would be looking for an answer. Jeremiah didn't
have one, and didn't seem to care. No purpose, no past, no future,
but an imagination and an artist's vision of life, wanting only for a
canvas to put his brush to.

Jeremiah sat down at his desk, because that is what you do when
you go to work, opened up a drawer and took out a yellow lined
pad, reached across the desk, sharpened a No. 2 Faber, rested it on
top of his pad, and then did nothing, in a spontaneous and uninhib-
ited way. He was waiting, waiting for some external force to push

or pull him this way or that, give him something to react to. If he sat long enough in one spot, Destiny for sure would arrive. And so it did in the person of Maynard E. Brown who was clearly made uncomfortable by Jeremiah's lackadaisical, breezy indifference to life's necessities. Maynard, who knew he was up against something difficult and in many ways dangerous, searched for the right words while trying to appear as spontaneous and relaxed as Jeremiah.

"So," he said, with bounce in his voice as he looked out the window. "Fog's lifting. A sunny day in the fifties. Nice day for some golf. Maybe we could leave early and play a round. How about you, Nick?"

"Sure," said Nick.

Jeremiah raised his eyebrows quizzically, but said nothing. He wasn't going to make this easy for Maynard, but then again he wasn't going to go out of his way to make it hard, either. He was just being who he was, more dead than alive.

"Jeremiah, we've got to talk," said Maynard, waiting for a response, which he didn't get. "It's not working. Something's broken. We've got to fix it."

"Not working?" asked Jeremiah. "You mean I am not walking on my hind legs like a trained poodle?"

"I mean you're not walking, period. You're not walking. You're not talking. You're not thinking. You're not writing. You're barely breathing. What the hell is going on?"

"I seem to have lost my capacity to lie," said Jeremiah.

"It'll come back," said Maynard nervously. "Jeremiah, we all need lies. They are our bread and butter. They are the stuff and substance of our lives. You can't change that."

"I don't want to change it. I'm not trying to change it," said Jeremiah. "All I know is I've seen the string attached to the waving hand and I've seen who is pulling it."

"Jeremiah, my God, man, what's got into you? We all know it's a lie. There's no problem with that. The problem is looking behind the lie to see what's there. No one is ever supposed to do that. Pandora's box, it must never be opened. That is the secret to life.

Those shadows on the wall. They are life. Damn it, Jeremiah. Get a hold of yourself."

Maynard was frightened. The lie of his life was seeping through the cracks of his awareness. Those cracks were getting harder and harder to block up and Jeremiah wasn't making it any easier.

"Listen, Jeremiah," he continued, "a lie masquerading as truth. I'll take that any day. That's what keeps us alive and in business. Forget about the rest. Come on. Get with it. I'll be in my office."

Jeremiah, saying nothing, continued to sit in his chair. Apparently Destiny hadn't gotten his attention. Jeremiah was patient. He would wait.

About ten minutes passed, then Maynard reappeared.

"All right. What's this truth business? What do you mean? What do you want to do?" asked Maynard.

"I haven't the foggiest idea."

"That's serious," said Maynard, wringing his hands. "That's serious. Damned serious. What the hell is going on here? Damn it," he said, almost in tears, and hurried off to his office again.

About twenty minutes later he appeared again, this time calmer.

"Jeremiah," he said affably, "what about the golf?"

"Sure," said Jeremiah.

"How about you Nick?" asked Maynard

"Sure," said Nick

The three men teed off around four o'clock. There were a couple of hours of daylight left. They pretty much had the course to themselves. Jeremiah, who was usually an erratic golfer, who could get off a beautiful shot with his three iron and then spend ten minutes hitting from one end of the green to the other with his putter, played relatively consistent golf and had a few good par holes. Maynard, who was a very good golfer, was off his game and though ahead of Jeremiah, played behind him on several holes. Maynard and Nick were pretty evenly matched, which meant that on this day, Nick was out in front.

The tee for the sixth hole was high above the green, down a narrow fairway bordered with tall trees and dense underbrush and straightaway at one hundred fifty yards. It was a good five-iron shot to the flag. Anything but a straight shot was a waste of time. Maynard set up the ball, placed his club behind it, adjusted his feet, wiggled his rear end, brought the club back slowly and evenly and then down at a slightly faster pace, shifting his weight to the front foot just a little too soon and then compensating by moving his swing to the left, resulting in a high hook that disappeared into the ruff.

"Damn," said Maynard.

Jeremiah set up his ball, addressed it in much the same way, brought his club back slowly and evenly, came down with a little faster pace, hit the ball squarely and brought his arms up and out in front of him in a beautiful follow-through. It was a perfect shot and landed on the green about five feet from the pin. Nick's ball landed right alongside Jeremiah's.

"Damn," said Maynard.

The three of them walked down the hill and into the rough in search of Maynard's ball and, surprisingly, actually found it between a rock and a hard place on some fallen leaves. Maynard had a clear line to the green if he hit a straight ball. If he didn't, he was liable to suffer serious injury, depending on which tree or rock the ball ricocheted off. He took a good deal of time addressing the ball and hit a perfectly straight shot that cleared all the obstacles. But it was too high to reach the green. Instead, it came with a slow roll to the edge of the water hole just in front of the green, had enough forward movement to make it over the hill and then come to a stop halfway down the grassy slope, about six inches above the water. This was a tough shot to take without getting one foot wet. Maynard accepted the challenge, but swung too hard, topped the ball and sent it straight into the center of the pond.

"Damn," said Maynard, taking his soggy left foot out of the water, climbing up the little incline. "Damn. I can't hit the ball. I don't want to hit the ball. I don't care about hitting it. Golf is white man's game."

He took his club, threw it halfway across the fairway and then sat down on the turf.

"I'm tired of being white," he said. "I've been white all my life, since the age of three when my mother taught me how to walk white. 'See white man over there?' she said. 'See how he's walking? See how his arms hang loosely at his side and are close to his body, moving gracefully back and forth? See how still his shoulders are? That's how I want you to walk. See that nigger over there, walking from side to side with his shoulders? White man walks from his knees. That nigger is walking with his shoulders. Don't ever let me catch you doing that.' I've been walking white ever since, walking like I have a full diaper and don't want anyone to know. I learned how to talk white, think white, and feel white. I'm tired of laughing off the top of my head instead of from my belly. I don't care about any of this shit you white people seem to think is so important. I never have.

"I wants to be black," said Maynard, starting to stretch out his words in a slow drawl. "I wants to git me a little farm in Vuhginya, and I wants to eats me some waaaawta melon," he said, singing out the words, "and spits the pits off the front porch from my rockin' chair. And I wants to walk down dem doit roads by the bogs and bayous. And I wants to sing me some spichul songs at the end of a long day hoin' mah corn. And my black momma be waitin' fo me at de doah, waving to me, as I walks up de pat to my little shack which is mah home. And day is lil' chillins, runnin' around. Day is mah granchillin.' And day runs to greet me when I comes up de road. And my soul fills up wid a beautiful song when ah see dem and picks dem up in mah arms. Ah is a happy man. Ah is a free man. Day ain't no white man to be seen fo miles and miles. We talks about white man at night time, drinkin' from a jug a corn whiskey. We talks about him wit pity in our heart and feah in our soul and thanks de Lawd dat we ain't white like him, dat we ain't lonely, misuhable and ignorant, dried up and dead, like the shell of an acorn after de squirrel done had his way wid it. We feah de white man who wants to destroy life wherever he goes. But we feels safe because we know we ain't got nottin' he wants."

Maynard stopped talking and turned to look at Jeremiah who was looking at him through slits in his eyes, shaking his head in disbelief and amusement as Maynard spoke, and then at Nick who, uncharacteristically, had a big, broad, happy smile on his face.

"Dats de story," said Maynard, returning to his old self, his old white self, now imitating white man imitating black man. "Dat de whole story. I want out," he said, exhaling deeply.

"What about Sissy?" asked Jeremiah.

"That's been over for a long time. In fact, it was over before it started. She married me to get back at her father. I married her to prove I was white. Once we made our points we had no use for each other."

"Maynard," said Jeremiah, "you're as white as I am. You're never going to be black. It's lost to you forever, just as lying is to me."

"Maybe yo is raht, Chemaya. But I's gonna die tryin'."

Things happened fast after that day on the golf course. There was a meeting at Maynard's place with Jeremiah, Maynard and Sissy and Nick attending.

"It's over," said Maynard, as he flipped a hamburger. "My life as a white man is over. I'm giving my share in the *Ledger* over to Sissy. The lies, the truth. It's all the same to me. You people decide. I'm worn out trying."

That was Sunday. On Monday, Maynard called everyone into his office. He was wearing some old dungarees with the cuffs turned up at the bottom and a blue denim work shirt. He brought with him a long stick. Tied at the end was a large red handkerchief which he had fashioned into a pouch that he used to carry five pair of underwear, his extra large jock strap, two pair of socks and his toothbrush, all the material possessions he was taking with him in his search for blackness.

"Bruthuz and sistuhs," he said, addressing the startled and confused faces, "I uz had it. I done finish bein' white. I done finish walkin' with my knees an' talkin' from behind my closed mout. I gonna open my mout real wide and sing to de Lawd. I gonna sing about de black man and his sufferin'. I gonna sing de black man's blues till de devil hisself gonna shed a teah."

69

"I heah you, brother," said Jeremiah.

"I done finish lying. I done finish stealing. I iz gonna sleep like a babe at nighttime and swim wit de fishes in de sea."

"Say Amen, brother. Say Amen," said Nick.

"I iz sad fo white man. I iz gonna cry fo him, too. Poh white man is de most misahable crechuh on de eoit. He even mo misahable den black man cauz white man done fogot how to sing. He done fogot how to dance."

"Poh, white man," said the cleaning lady. "Poh, white man."

"De soul o' white man is gonna ROAST in hell," said Maynard, with fire in his voice.

"Oh, NO!" cried the cleaning lady. "Oh, NOOOO!"

"He gonna ROAST in hell fo all de bad he done, fo de babes he done burned, fo de lies he done told, fo de trees he done cut down, fo de air and de waters he done made foul wit his poisonous breat. But woist of all, he gonna roast because he done stole de Woid, he done snatched de Woid out a de hands a de Lawd Hisself, he done took it and done sullied it wit de slime from his mout. He done made de Woid doity. And fo dat de Lawd will nevuh fogive him," said Maynard in a hush, "nevuh."

With that Maynard picked up his stick with the red handkerchief at the end and as an afterthought took his nameplate off his office door and put it in his back pocket. Without turning around to say good-bye, he walked down the stairs and out of the door of the *North Benware Star Ledger*. That is the last that was seen of Maynard E. Brown, who is black.

CHAPTER 14

September 29, 2003

FIRST THING IN THE morning, Sissy called Jeremiah into her office. "Jeremiah," she said, "I am going to give you a shot at this. Let's see what you can come up with. You'll be on your own for the first month or so. Then we'll take stock."

Apparently, Sissy had not been apprised of Jeremiah's state of being. He had no vision for his own life. How would he manage to provide a vision for the *North Benware Star Ledger*? Jeremiah was fully aware that he was the wrong choice, but didn't know how to go about turning down an offer that only two years ago, waiting on tables, he could only have dreamt of. So, he accepted.

Jeremiah's first initiative as editor-in-chief was to get rid of Maynard's oversize desk and turn the office into a staff room where people could congregate for lunch and informal discussions. Some easy chairs, a couple of coffee tables, maybe even a small pool table would turn the room into a place to have some fun and relax.

"Having fun and relaxing is part of life. Why can't we do it at work?" Jeremiah asked the assembled personnel at his first official staff meeting. Did people want board games like Monopoly and Trivial Pursuit or would they rather play Bridge and Canasta? Should there be time set aside for just reading and another time for casual conversation? Should they bring in an outside consultant to give them some ideas and maybe even run the program? These are just some of the questions raised by Jeremiah and the others. The meeting was a grand success. Meryl volunteered to set up a schedule for activities in the room. It was decided to buy a small refrigerator and a microwave oven, to have a list of takeout menus rated according to mean time of delivery, mean temperature of the food at the time of arrival in degrees Celsius, and courtesy of the delivery persons. By a vote of twenty to two, with one abstention, it was decided to call the room "Chez Maynard," in memory of Maynard E. Brown, whom they had cordially resented when he was around and had grown to like more and more the less they saw of him.

A month or so passed and soon everyone was adjusted to the new routine and feeling pretty good about it. Jeremiah gave very little thought to the actual business of running the newspaper, that is to say of collecting news and printing it. The paper seemed to be doing fine on its own, so why should he get in the way? On a temporary basis he decided to cover funerals and charity balls. He assigned Meryl to weddings, and he asked the cleaning lady to write a column on cooking. He had once tasted some of her ribs. They were excellent.

Jeremiah himself was seated across the chessboard from Barry Upshaw at 11:30 A.M. on a rainy morning in early November. There was quiet conversation going on around him. Barry was suggesting to Jeremiah that it might be a good idea to do a series on family life, when a figure appeared in the doorway. At first Jeremiah didn't recognize her, so absorbed was he in his thoughts. Then he did. It was none other than Sissy Black, who is white. She looked none too pleased.

"Jeremiah, I'd like to speak to you in your office," she said tersely.

Jeremiah excused himself and led her to his desk behind the filing cabinets.

"This is your office?" she asked with raised eyebrows.

"Yes," said Jeremiah innocently.

"Who's in charge here?" she asked, her two arms supporting the weight of her body against the desk, her eyes staring into Jeremiah's.

"We all are," he said.

"Who's your proofreader?"

"There is none. We each proof our own copy."

"Read this," she said, slapping a copy of the previous day's paper onto his desk. "Second column. Second paragraph. Read it."

"'Yes day, an eight year old man was found Police estimate is body had been floating in the Raritan River Four years ago.'"

"It's gibberish Jeremiah. What's going on? The paper is filled with nonsense like that. There is no editorial direction. Someone has to be in charge."

"What's wrong with collective vision?"

"It lacks focus. That's what's wrong. And it's boring, Jeremiah. The name of the paper is the *North Benware Star Ledger*. There are some seventy-five hundred families living in North Benware. I think we ought to give them the community paper they want, which is what the *Ledger* was before Maynard got carried away with his grand ideas. We should be writing honest stories about local life. We should be interviewing local merchants about the new mall, interviewing school board members about this year's budget. There are some old people who know something about North Benware before it was North Benware. There are some local artists, a few playwrights and someone who owns a chain of two hundred motels nationwide. We should be writing about them. There is even local corruption. The board of supervisors is missing $50,000. They think the mayor used taxpayer money to help pay a gambling debt. Those are the stories we should be printing."

Jeremiah was hearing but he wasn't listening. Sissy was right, he knew that, but he just wasn't interested. Sissy could tell she wasn't getting through.

"Jeremiah, suppose we start doing some feature stories, some thoughtful writing on topics of general interest. No more trivia. No more scoops."

"Sure," he said.

"Good," said Sissy. "I'll be in my office."

She stopped and turned.

"Jeremiah," she said, "are you all right? You don't seem your old self. Have you ever thought of seeing a therapist?"

At first, he felt defensive. Then he realized that it wouldn't be such a bad idea. After all, he had been going through a lot these past months. Wouldn't this be the ideal person to help him get back on track?

"I'll think about it," he said.

The following week he scheduled an appointment.

Dr. Edwin Nostrum had his practice in the 70's, off Madison Avenue. His office was on the second floor, toward the back of the building and away from street noise. Nostrum was short and over-weight with a mass of uncombed, long gray hair. He breathed heavily.

"How are you today?" Nostrum asked in a friendly, casual way.

"Fine," said Jeremiah, winking with his right eye.

Nostrum noted the wink.

Jeremiah went on to tell him everything that had been happening. He told him Nick's remark about the "Blue Tie" story and how he had found that so demoralizing and how that led to the "Clearforest-Brickbat" story, a gun to his head and a trip to Florida. He told Nostrum about his experience with homeless man in Hard Times Square. He told him about his confusion over the truth and the lie and how he honestly couldn't tell one from the other anymore. How he couldn't stop lying but felt anguished every time he did.

"When I asked you how you were," observed Nostrum, "you said 'fine' and then winked with your right eye. What is that about?"

"Oh, that," said Jeremiah. "I do that all the time. When I lie, I wink. I can't help it."

"How long has that been going on?"

Jeremiah told him everything he could remember going back to when he was nine years old and the story he had made up about Bobby Grimes.

"And that's when your mother took you to a therapist."

"Yes."

"What was that like?"

"I don't remember much. I remember his office. I remember sitting in a big leather chair."

"And that's when you began winking."

"Yes. Can you fix it? Can you make an honest man out of me?"

"Jeremiah, I might be able to fix the wink. I doubt I can make an honest man out of you."

Nostrum rolled his chair over to where Jeremiah was sitting.

"Do you see that picture on the wall behind me?"

"Yes," said Jeremiah.

"Good. Do you see the handle of the cup?"

"Yes," said Jeremiah.

"Good. I want you to concentrate on that handle and not take your eyes off it."

Jeremiah did as he was told.

"You can hear me but you can't see me," said Nostrum. "I am looking at your left hand. I am staring at it. I can see it rising on its own with no help from you. You cannot stop it. Your hand is starting to move on its own. Little by little it is rising. That is good. Your hand is getting higher and higher. Very good. Now your hand is starting to get heavy, very heavy, too heavy to hold up. It is starting to move downward, very slowly, very slowly. When it touches the arm of your chair you will be asleep. Good, Jeremiah. Very good. Can you hear me?"

"Yes," said Jeremiah.

"Good. Now I want you to imagine yourself in Allworth's office and I want you to tell me everything that happens."

Word for word, Jeremiah repeated the entire session.

"Okay, Jeremiah, now I want you to make up a scene for me, create a place where you will be happier than you ever have been. You can make it anything you want it to be."

Jeremiah thought for a moment.

"I am naked. I am jumping up and down on a trampoline. I am surrounding by beautiful women with magnificent breasts. They are all naked jumping up and down the way I am."

"That's it? That's your favorite place?" asked Nostrum skeptically.

"Yes," said Jeremiah, "that's it."

"Okay, Jeremiah, every time you lie that is where you will be, jumping on your trampoline surrounded by bouncing breasts. No longer will you be tormented when you lie. You will feel happy and free. Every time you lie, you will smile. Do you understand, Jeremiah?"

"Yes," said Jeremiah with a broad smile on his face. "I understand."

"Good," said Nostrum. "Now I am going to count from one to ten. Count after me, one number at a time. When we get to ten you will be awake. You will forget everything that just happened."

Jeremiah opened his eyes. He remembered nothing of what he had just experienced. The broad smile on his face would not go away. He had never felt happier.

CHAPTER 15

November 2003

A LMOST IMMEDIATELY, JEREMIAH WAS transported, flooded with ideas for great stories. But there would be a difference this time. Jeremiah wouldn't be lying for fame or for expediency. He would be lying for the sheer beauty of it. This would be pure lying, lying which showed no regard for the truth whatsoever, that in its freedom and imagination was akin to poetry, philosophy, subatomic physics and some of the greatest chewing gum jingles ever written.

One of his first stories, the one which brought him to the attention of some of the most important and powerful people in this country, was a story of modest proportions but brilliant insight which really wasn't a lie in the literal sense but nonetheless did violence to the truth in a way that was subtle, whimsical and engaging. It was entitled, "Poverty and Cholesterol Levels." In this thoughtful

and provocative little piece, Jeremiah started with the simple observation that people who are poor have low cholesterol levels. This
important fact, which is intuitively true – poor people lack the
resources to purchase ice cream, butter, milk, eggs and beef –
Jeremiah took the trouble to demonstrate by means of extensive
data he had collected from some of the poorest and worst-run hos-
pitals in the city, then generalizing the epidemiological implications
through sound reasoning and well-developed arguments, drawing
the obvious conclusion in his final paragraph that "poverty is good
for the health," i.e., it keeps cholesterol down.

Here was a piece of high level, sophisticated investigation more
akin to some of the most advanced academic research than the usual
journalistic claptrap. And it did not go unappreciated for its true
worth. Quite the contrary.

The article was an immediate success and was quoted in medical
and social work journals across the country. Things began crackling
once again at the *North Benware Star Ledger*. Readership picked up
considerably, but it was a different readership. This new kind of rarefied lying did not have mass appeal. But it was cherished and coveted by an intellectual and academic elite who owed its power to
the driving wish of the average American to be led blindly off the
highest cliff by a team of self-proclaimed experts.

Jeremiah's name was on the lips of some of the richest and most
indolent people in the country. He was the topic of conversation at
the finest restaurants and bars, at polo and tennis matches, at fox
hunts and regattas, charity balls, masked balls, corporate dining
rooms, faculty dining rooms from Harvard to the University of
Small Minds in Southern Illinois, and at exclusive dinner parties on
Park Avenue, south of Ninety-Sixth Street and north of Grand
Central Station.

It certainly would not be an exaggeration to say that Jeremiah
began taking himself seriously – perhaps too much so – for the first
time in his life. In the good old days, his shirt collar was always
opened, he was never in a hurry, always had time for an anecdote
or a digression, was as good a listener as he was a talker, would just

as willingly take the long way round as he would a short cut. This was all true because basically he didn't give a damn. And it showed, and it was such a pleasant relief from all those people around him who never had time to sniff the steaming coffee. Now Jeremiah was one of them. His style of dress changed, as did his way of walking, talking, smiling, laughing and coughing. His vocabulary and diction changed, as did the inflection in his voice.

He began saying, "Oh, really" and "I suspect" – as in "I suspect it's going to be a warm day" – quite often, and began lisping his initial S's. Instead of "again," rhyming with "hen," Jeremiah would say "again," rhyming with "rain."

Before his "Poverty and Cholesterol" story, Jeremiah had talked in an easygoing, rambling way, sloshing the words about in his mouth and savoring them as if he were tasting a fine Bordeaux before swallowing it. Now he spoke in clipped phrases with a staccato beat, swallowing his words as if they were cod-liver oil, and emphasizing his points with sharp, angular movements of his hands. Jeremiah began buying his clothes at the finest shops in Manhattan with the invaluable assistance of his wife, Emma, who was finally coming into her own now that Jeremiah had become connected to big money. Although she had poor taste concerning her own dress, she was very astute in buying for Jeremiah everything he needed to convey the image of wealth, status and prestige, which she had all along coveted and devoted so much of her time to studying.

Emma fussed over Jeremiah's attire and would think nothing of spending $300 on a shirt or $150 on a tie. She had his suits made to order for him in Hong Kong, after his measurements had been taken by an Indian from Calcutta in a Howard Johnson's Motel on Eighth Avenue.

For the first time in the marriage the couple was beginning to work as a team. Jeremiah was getting the attention and devotion he had always wanted. Emma was getting what she wanted. In her mind, her regime of indoctrinating Jeremiah with the benefits of getting and spending had finally born fruit.

So when Emma asked Jeremiah what he thought about her

approaching Sissy Black for advice on how to conduct herself in this new social milieu that Jeremiah had inadvertently opened up for her, he could honestly and enthusiastically respond "Smashing" and mean it, as much as he had ever meant anything.

"It isn't as if I'm trying to sneak in the back door," she said, talking to herself in the mirror as she applied some lipstick, "or pass for someone I'm not."

"No," said Jeremiah, tucking his shirt into his trousers, "it is more like someone trying to learn how to play tennis for the first time, who needs to be taught everything from how to dress to how to walk on the court and which side of the net to play from."

"Exactly," said Emma, putting the cap on her lipstick.

And Sissy, who was now unattached, was delighted at the opportunity to spend some time with Emma. For though she and Emma were from dramatically different backgrounds, they shared in common a distaste for weak men whom they nonetheless courted perhaps, they would argue, because there was no other kind to be found.

Seated at a small table at an overpriced gourmet eatery on Madison Avenue, in the eighties, on the west side of the street, famous in the city and perhaps the world over for sticks of bread baked in special ovens and sold anywhere good food is sold for $2.50 each, where casually dressed men and women in their thirties and forties munch on $13 chicken salad sandwiches, Sissy and Emma had their first training session.

"Smile as little as possible. Never laugh or show enthusiasm and never ask the price of anything," advised Sissy one snappy afternoon in late November as the wind was whipping up the scattered papers outside the plate glass window.

"Don't try and pretend you're one of them. They'll never buy it and will be insulted."

Several tables away, with an extremely handsome, well-dressed young man twenty years her junior, probably a gay model, was Tracy Blount, an acquaintance of Sissy's. The two women acknowledged each other with a slight rise of the eyebrow and an ever-so-slight nod of the head.

"Did you see what I just did. That is how the wealthy communicate. Very subtle, much of it is nonverbal. There's no, 'Hey, Tracy! How's it goin?' None of that. My best advice to you is to say as little as possible, especially at the beginning."

Emma asked some questions concerning locution. Sissy said she was moving too fast. Both agreed that the session was a success and set the date for the next one, which was to take place at the Palm Court Room at the Plaza.

CHAPTER 16

Early December 2003

EMMA DIDN'T HAVE TO wait long to put into practice what she had learned. The first week in December she and Jeremiah were invited for "an evening" at the Watsons' of Park Avenue and 73rd Street. In her own hand, on the inside of a very elegant note card, addressed to Emma herself, Betsy Watson requested the presence of "you and your husband, for whom we all have such great admiration, for an evening of light food and conversation. Dress is casual." Nick Belladonna – Jeremiah's trusted friend and political advisor – received his own invitation, though without the personal flourish. Sissy was invited as well.

Emma, of course, was delighted. But intuitively understanding that the rich – who make fine distinctions concerning their social events, differentiating between levels of "lightness" and "casualness," whose gradations can vary from one part of the country to another – spoke a language different from hers, she sought Sissy's assistance in deciphering the invitation.

Sissy knew at once that arrival time was around 7 P.M. and departure around 10:30 P.M., an early departure, probably because the Watsons were leaving for an excursion to Switzerland the next day, that pasta would be served, that wearing a dress would be inappropriate and that Cawley Watson probably had politics on his mind and wished his wife to create an evening of casual discussion which he could lead in that direction should he so choose.

Cawley Watson – whom Jeremiah knew to be a prominent and powerful presidential backer – was of the Watsons of Delaware, a family of industrialists who, at the turn of the century, had invented the chemical used to make the common mouthwash blue. His father, a stern, bespectacled Methodist, had turned this insignificant discovery into a large fortune which his son, Cawley, had done his very best to dissipate, with surprisingly little success.

Betsy Watson, née Krusky-Von-Auswich, the mere mention of which name opened the doors to some of the most decadent households in Europe, a Hungarian of Austrian descent who claimed she could trace her lineage back to the Hapsburgs, had a fine operatic voice which she sometimes displayed at one of her "evenings of music." She came with a modest dowry of close to fifteen million dollars and a remarkable collection of eighteenth-century napkin rings.

When Jeremiah arrived home, Emma, beside herself with excitement, read him the invitation in breathless gasps.

"Oh" was all Jeremiah said, having on very short notice and with remarkable ease adapted himself to the ways of the rich.

"But, *liebling*, do you know what this means?" asked Emma, twirling about in her housecoat and pantoufles like a sixteen-year-old who had been asked to her first prom. "Do you know what it means?"

"It means you're going to be flitting around like a monkey on amphetamines for the next two weeks. I suspect that's what it means," said Jeremiah indulgently as Emma covered half her face with a dishtowel and did her best imitation of a belly dance to the tune of "They don't wear pants on the sunny side of France."

Formal socializing had never been Jeremiah's strong suit. He would find it easier to change his diction and dress than to master his distaste for cocktail party conversation. He much preferred a chat on a park bench, or a good laugh over a hamburger and beer at a local pub to an overpriced and mediocre meal at a classy restaurant or a formal dinner in the home of the wealthy, which in essence this was, Betsy Watson's protestations to the contrary notwithstanding.

"This is going to be boring," said Jeremiah to Nick, the evening of the event, waiting for Emma to dress, himself dressed in a fine Gucci belt and fine Gucci shoes, a made-to-order 100 percent Egyptian cotton shirt, his hand-tailored Harris Tweed jacket and his worsted wool slacks, really looking quite handsome to himself as he studied his image in the mirror.

"Oh, Jeremiah, don't be such a stick in the mud," said Emma glowingly on her way from the bathroom to the bedroom, giving him a peck on the cheek as she paused to examine her appearance. "I think this Cawley Watson likes you. He has money and influence. You should get to know him."

Jeremiah knew she was right but wished there were another way to go about it. He pulled at his shirt cuff until he was satisfied it was showing just the right amount beyond his jacket sleeve.

"Well?" she asked, standing beside him as they both looked into the mirror.

"You look elegant," said Jeremiah, almost admiringly. "You look quite elegant."

"Emma, you have outdone yourself," said Nick.

Dressed in a black silk blouse, open at the neck, gold earrings and a gold choker, loose-fitting black, velvet slacks, her hair nicely sculpted to the shape of her head, indeed she did look elegant. Sissy would be proud.

CHAPTER 17

Later That Evening

THE FOUR GUESTS ARRIVED fashionably late, as Sissy had instructed Emma, that is to say, about twenty minutes past the pre-
scribed arrival time. They were greeted at the door of the Watson
apartment building by a uniformed doorman who sought their
names on a guest list. They were escorted through a long, richly
furnished lobby to the mahogany-paneled elevator operated by a
white-gloved young Irishman who accompanied them to the door
of the Watson apartment. An Asian man in his sixties greeted them
on behalf of the Watsons and then presented them to Betsy Watson
herself.

"How nice of you to come," said Betsy to Emma as she shook her
hand.

Emma gave a modest smile, nodded a greeting and, to her credit, said not a word, and by so doing raised herself in the eyes of her hostess, who was prepared to expect the worst.

Turning to Jeremiah, Betsy said, "I can't tell you how pleased we are to welcome you into our home."

To which Jeremiah replied, in his best imitation of Bryn Mawr malocclusion, Scarsdale lockjaw, Cambridge umbrage and Buckley whine, "Quite."

This by no means modest response on Jeremiah's part had an unsettling effect on Betsy Watson, who was doing her best to ease the Greenfields into the upper reaches with as little discomfort as possible. Here was Jeremiah cold-cocking at the very moment when her guard, almost always up, was actually down.

"You must be Nick," said Betsy, in words dipped in ice, from behind her Plexiglas shield. "How nice of you to come."

"This is my friend, Janet Brody," said Nick.

Betsy had clearly been put off balance by Jeremiah's manner, and actually lost her footing on the deep pile carpet as she turned to escort her guests to the living room. At this moment her husband came to her rescue, the kind of thing upper-class couples do for each other in social situations and, with a gesture of his arm, offered Jeremiah a greeting which, within this particular context, all things being relative, might almost have been considered "hearty."

"Why, Jeremiah," he said, as if Jeremiah and he had been room-mates at college and were seeing each other for the first time in twenty years, "this is grand." Then, clapping his hand on Jeremiah's shoulder, he walked him through the twenty-by-thirty-foot foyer in the direction of the forty-by-sixty-foot living room where the guests were gathered, while Betsy and Emma, following some five or six paces behind, engaged in the kind of chatter which women engage in when they are out of the earshot of men and which seems to know no social barriers. As for Nick, with some beluga caviar on a wedge of cucumber between his lips, and a martini in either hand, he settled himself into the middle of the most comfortable available couch alongside Janet, provocatively ignoring the young woman seated next to him.

Cawley Watson, for his part, was really not, considering his status and upbringing, a boring person. Yet he suffered from an affliction – indications of which have been confined to wealthy WASPs who spend too much time sailing – known as aridity. He had an extremely dry way of talking, dry in the way that skin is dry, skin that has been exposed too long to the elements. The sounds came out cracked and crumbling – like the page of an old text that falls apart as it is touched – reaching the listener's ears like motes in the eye, irritating and inescapable.

Stopping for a moment at the threshold of the living room and turning to address Jeremiah directly, he said, "Jeremiah, I admire your writing. That 'Poverty and Cholesterol' piece was brilliant. I am grateful for the opportunity to be telling you this in person and I am honored that you decided to come tonight.

"You know it is rare to find someone who can misappropriate the truth with such flair and devotion. I don't know what your background is or how you came about this gift which usually is confined to the better universities, the board rooms of large corporations and the hidden recesses of Washington power politics, but you are truly a genius, whether you know it or not."

Jeremiah couldn't help but be flattered, though he wasn't as overcome as he might have been in the past. He was trying his hardest to like this person who was doing his best to please him but found the smell of Watson's breath distasteful, the crackling of his words assaultive, and the sight of his watery blue eyes, which conveyed not a hint of soulfulness, most unsettling.

Jeremiah was beginning to wonder, as he told Nick later, what in the name of common sense he was doing at such a gathering. He had not the slightest regret about toying with the truth in any which way he chose, but it disturbed him to see that these were the people he was writing for. He realized, as does any artist when confronted with an admiring public, that not one of them would understand the beauty, meaning and purpose that lying had for him, and hence that none of them was in a position to validate him for the artist he was.

"Thank you, Mr. Watson," said Jeremiah casually, abandoning the affectation with which he had begun the evening.

"Oh, Jeremiah, call me Cawley, please," said Watson, in a gesture of friendship. Then he turned to wait for Emma and his wife, who would do the introductions.

Emma had never looked better than she did at that moment. Her shoulders squared off, her chin held high, she walked beside Betsy Watson, her eyes focused on the two men as if this were the day of her marriage and Betsy was about to give her away to Jeremiah. Jeremiah took her hand as they began the rounds.

CHAPTER 18

The Same Evening

AS THE GROUP NOTICED the presence of the Greenfields on the threshold of the room, chatter came to a halt and all eyes were on Jeremiah and his wife, heavy-lidded eyes, sunken eyes, bloodshot eyes, eyes that wandered and found no resting place, eyes of disdain.

Starting on her left and working her way around the room, Betsy introduced Jeremiah and Emma to each of the couples, one at a time, each couple rising as if to receive a diploma and a handshake, as their name was announced.

"These are the Letchworths, Lindsay and Lester."

"Delighted," said Lester Letchworth, who had known Cawley Watson since their days at Andover.

"Charmed," said his wife, Lindsay, her lip curled in a half snarl.

"These are the Reerdons, Falconer and Philatele," said Betsy, moving to the next couple.

A silver-haired, ruddy-faced and distinguished-looking gentleman stood up and greeted the Greenfields in most distinctivetones. He was an amateur actor. Summertime he played Caesar at the Hamptons.

Next came Sissy, in the company of a gangly, socially inept banker from Topeka, Kansas.

"Hullo," he said, giving Jeremiah and Emma each a hearty handshake.

"And this is Smythe Johnson," said Betsy, to the youngest guest, probably mid to late thirties, a moody but intelligent-looking chap, who responded to Betsy's introduction with a "hi" and a wave of his hand, failing to rise as the others had done, thus conveying his impatience with the formalities rather than with the Greenfields themselves.

"And with him," said Betsy, with obvious disapproval, to a strikingly beautiful black woman, "is his friend, Amanda Jones. She works as a teacher in a private school on the West Side."

Amanda rose, smiled a most beautiful smile and looked straight into Jeremiah's eyes.

"How lovely," he said.

"And this," said Betsy with particular pride, obviously relishing his presence and conveying in her tone that she was sure Jeremiah would as well, "is Jonathan Stately, professor of political science at Princeton, author of a recently published, full-length study entitled, *Gullibility and the American Way of Life*. And this is his wife, Tricia," concluded Betsy, freeing Jeremiah and Emma to mingle with the guests.

Jonathan, who had already had a few, made a gesture of rising, thought better of it, satisfied the etiquette of the occasion with a "Pleased to meet you," drawing out the "e" of "pleased" considerably beyond what the occasion called for, his fattened tongue catching on the preceding "l."

Tricia, having rearranged her hair and hemline for Jeremiah's benefit, gave him a riveting stare, pulled him down beside her on the couch and said, in musically captivating tones in an accent somewhere out of Tennessee, her soft, warm, gentle hand continuing to hold his, "I'll bet you could use a drink."

Jeremiah accepted, intoxicated already by the smell of Tricia's perfume, the caress of her hand, the pressure of her thigh against his, and her unshod foot against his calf.

The introductions thus completed, the evening could begin in earnest, which it did, with the same backbiting one would expect to find at a social meeting of the middle class. Except there was one difference. Unlike the middle class who, at a similar gathering, would break down into two groups along sexual lines for purposes of vilifying their respective spouses, the rich, who have always recognized married life for the sham it is, complain about "the help," which means everyone and anyone who does for the rich what the rich choose not to do for themselves.

"I think Fong has been eating the caviar," says Mama Watson.

"He's been sitting in my chair," says Papa Watson. "It's time for him to go."

For fifteen years it has been time for Fong to go. Yet he stays just where he is. He knows that the rich need him more than he needs the rich. He knows that his real function is not to serve but to provide status, and that he will receive an especially generous Christmas bonus if he misbehaves just a little, supplying fire for the Watson cannon in their conversations with their other wealthy friends who are always trying to outdo the Watsons in their stories about "the help."

But the wealthy, unlike the lower classes, who are continually sniping at those above and below them, reserve their greatest enmity for those of their own, regardless of sex, who fail to bear the mantle of wealth with proper pomposity and self-righteousness. There are fierce loyalties and rivalries based almost exclusively on geography, including, but not limited to, place of birth, principal residence, summer home and, of course, acquaintances.

"Did you see whom Charles Hastings was with last night at Theodore's?" asked Lindsay Letchworth. Charles, it so happens, had been with a West Sider – old uptown money has nothing but disdain for the West Side – a hard-driven, bleached-blond, well-tanned (old money is usually ashen) owner of a chain of fast food restaurants. "And did you see what she was wearing?"

"Obviously off the rack at Bloomingdales," interjected Philatele Reerdon.

"Well, you know Charles," said her husband, Falconer, expansively.

"That's exactly my point," pursued Lindsay.

"Of course, this kind of thing is to be expected," observed Lester Letchworth philosophically, "when there is a divorce."

"Such a middle-class thing to do," observed Philatele, back arched, brows raised, lids lowered, as she reached for a caviar canape.

"I kind of like Charles," said Smythe Johnson, tossing one of the throw pillows into the air. "He's an excellent tennis player."

"It's not a question of tennis, Smythe. There is something more serious at stake here," said Lester Letchworth in a patronizing tone.

"And what could that be?" asked Smythe, turning to look at his interlocutor.

Recognizing that things were about to get out of hand, Betsy Watson immediately interposed herself between Smythe and Lester by changing the subject and addressing Emma. Her response, though quick and supple, was almost not quick enough, for in the highly rarefied atmosphere of old uptown money, the slightest variation in air mixture can result in an explosion.

Introducing the Greenfields was a risk. Betsy knew that. Smythe Johnson, set off balance by their presence, had been on the verge of expressing contempt for his class, a contempt which under the proper circumstances was modulated in such a way as to produce a gentle cynicism that was part of what many found charming in his manner. He was about to lose that charm by indulging in the kind of direct confrontation that old uptown money never allows itself on any occasion.

"I understand you're quite a baker," said Betsy to Emma solicitously, almost enviously, the helpless victim of self-defining class

92

constraints, wanting nothing more than to boil an egg, arrange a pile of linens, or wash a floor, feeling deprived of these opportunities by birth and resenting the middle class for having them.

"Sank wou," said Emma, who reverted to baby talk on those occasions when she was out of her element.

"Say, what?" said Falconer Reerdon with a furrow of disdain on his brow.

"Fong!" said Betsy with a piercing ring to her voice, revealing just a bit of frenzy beneath her well-composed facade. "Fong!" she repeated, rising from her chair. "Set for dinner. Now!" commanding as she would a well-trained Labrador retriever.

Fong appeared, unflustered.

"Yes, Madame," he said, bowing slightly as he always did when there were guests present.

"Set for dinner, please!" Betsy said again, in an overly controlled, lowered voice, clenching her upper molars against the lower.

"Yes, Madame," said Fong again with another slight bow.

An uneasy quiet settled over the group. Each person had a clear sense of what he could do wrong. No one seemed to know how to get things back on the right footing. Betsy was clearly in need of some help. Emma, realizing she had erred and wanting to recoup her losses, began to speak. Sissy cut her off.

"Falconer," said Sissy, "tell us that story about your trip to Africa as a stowaway when you were sixteen."

"That's a bore," said Smythe Johnson, enjoying the role of spoiler, which Betsy had shortly before taken away from him.

"I'll bet Jeremiah has a few tales to tell," said Tricia Stately, her hand resting on Jeremiah's thigh as she spoke.

This seemed to please the group. After all, meeting Jeremiah was the unspoken purpose of this get-together.

"Yes," joined in Cawley Watson. "You know so much about Washington, about our president. Let us hear what you have to say. I don't mean the crumbs you throw to the riffraff. We want to know the president's underpinnings, his way of thinking, his philosophy of life."

To the best of his knowledge, the president had no underpinnings or philosophy of life. True to his instincts, however, Jeremiah understood that Cawley and the rest of them wanted to hear something unbelievable that they could believe in. He gave them exactly what they wanted.

"The president is no ordinary man," Jeremiah began, disengaging Tricia's hand from his thigh and rising from the couch to address the group. "He's a man of principle, a simple man, a man of strong conviction, a man of ambition, and a man of courage who would rather insult his wife about her cooking than swallow a piece of over-seasoned chicken.

"The president is a real man, a real American man, a man who believes in truth, in justice, in the American way of life and in the God-given right of the oil cartel to charge whatever it pleases for a barrel of oil."

This drew enthusiastic applause.

"The president would never harm a flea. But he will not back down from shedding another man's blood to advance his own cause or the cause of his brothers and sisters, the cause of people like those I see in this room, people with high breeding who understand the meaning of indolence, people of unprincipled self-devotion, for whom no indulgence is too great, no pleasure too small."

More applause and quite a few "hear, hears."

"People of blood must support the president. For if the average middle-class American ever sees the system for the hoax it is," said Jeremiah in conclusion, "the game of polo will never be the same."

Rising as if one, the group applauded.

"Bravo, Jeremiah," said Cawley Watson, placing his arm around Jeremiah's shoulder. "That was brilliant. Fine work, my friend. Fine work."

The others pressed towards Jeremiah with hands extended in gestures of congratulation, smiling broadly, chattering animatedly amongst themselves.

Fong, who had been waiting patiently on the sidelines for

Jeremiah to finish his remarks, directed guests to the dining room where plates of cold pasta, salmon mousse, and seared foie gras on a bed of frisé vinaigrette were spread elegantly across the table. The evening ended with Betsy Watson doing a lovely rendition of the "Bell Song" from *Lakmé*.

CHAPTER 19

Two Days Later

JEREMIAH, WHO UP TO this point had been something of a mythic figure in the eyes of his admirers, now took on a real-life presence that
equaled and maybe even surpassed the myth itself, a myth that
Jeremiah himself had done very little to create. For Jeremiah was not
a myth-maker or a narcissistic zealot, he was a simple liar toiling in
the vineyards of deceit, practicing a craft for which he was justifiably
appreciated and honored.

Word got around about Jeremiah's success at the Watsons' and
now everyone wanted a piece of the action. The invitations multiplied. Central Park South, Central Park West, Fifth and Madison
avenues all put in a bid for Jeremiah. And Jeremiah did his best to
oblige, difficult as it was to accept an invitation from one side of
town without offending the other.

There was a perfumed note from Tricia Stately and an invitation for Nick and Jeremiah to have lunch with Cawley Watson at the Upper East Side Club for Gentlemen of Wealth and Status, which Jeremiah accepted along with Nick. Over beef Wellington and Nuits St. Georges, Jeremiah and Nick were introduced to a group of well-dressed, well-heeled elderly gentlemen, all of whom smoked cigars and drank cognac, all of whom conveyed their support for Jeremiah and expressed an interest in seeing him enter political life. Taking him aside – Jeremiah motioned to Nick to follow – to an unoccupied, oak-paneled, leather-upholstered library with imposing portraits of self-satisfied men of wealth and status adorning its walls, Cawley addressed Jeremiah in somber tones.

"Jeremiah," he said confidentially, "I'm going to be honest with you. I'm worried. I don't know if the president can go the distance. He is not much of a performer. And as you and I both know, that is what the office is about.

"We might need help in '04. I can see you playing a role. I'm not sure what yet. But I want you to think seriously about making the greatest sacrifice a man can make for his country, allowing himself to be humiliated in the pursuit of higher office. I'm not saying it will happen. But it might and I want you to be ready with an answer if we decide we need you."

Jeremiah thanked Cawley for paying him such homage and said he would give it serious thought. He would accept, of course. But as Nick and Jeremiah were walking down Fifth Avenue, caught up in the flow of shoppers, strollers and toilers after having bid Cawley and his friends farewell, the magnitude of what lay before him started settling into his consciousness.

"It is one thing to daydream about being president," said Jeremiah, stopping to look into the window at the Bonwit men's shop, "it is quite something else considering it as a practical reality. What would I wear to my press conferences? What kind of jokes would I tell? What would be the presidential style by which I would be known to history?"

Nick studied Jeremiah as he peered into the store window and spoke his thoughts aloud. Was he really standing beside the future president of the United States? Was this the way it really happened?

CHAPTER 20

Christmas Week 2003

WHILE ACTIVELY INVOLVED IN preparing for his hypothetical candidacy, Jeremiah continued to fulfill his role as writer and editor-in-chief for the *North Benware Star Ledger*. He had an admiring public to serve, and serve them he did, feeding them an abundance of outrageous concoctions, each one more far-fetched than the next. But the story that capped it all was probably his most ingenious ever. Few writers of any caliber would have even thought of attempting it.

Jeremiah chose an issue that was ridiculous and transformed it into something inconsequential, thereby enriching the political dialogue and winning the respect and admiration of both Aristotelians and Platonists. Like any great creation, it was a question of the right man at the right time.

Hasn't every thoughtful American wondered at one point in his or her life, if there is, indeed, a difference between Republicans and Democrats? Jeremiah did more than just wonder. He actually came up with an answer. And he wasn't satisfied with empty generalizations or witty barbs. No. He dished up some hard facts.

Jeremiah researched, in depth and at length, every member of both houses of Congress, drawing on unknown biographical resources, unpublished letters, speeches, writings, interviews, voting records and bathroom graffiti. He outlined, categorized, analyzed, synthesized and processed every bit of material he had collected in search of those attributes that would serve to differentiate the two parties. And he came up with nothing. By means of regression equations, two-factor fixed-effects analysis of variance with unequal N's, chi squares, T-tests and Tyne tests, he established and then compared "mean level of corruption and dishonesty," "marital devotion quotient," and "ratio of hypocrisy to cowardice." He used line graphs, bar graphs and polygraphs, pie charts, cake charts and eye charts. And got nowhere. But he didn't give up.

"There must be a difference," he said to Nick one morning, pacing back and forth in front of his desk, tossing a football up in the air as he walked, pausing every so often to drop back for a pass or dodge a few tacklers. Then it occurred to him.

"Of course," he shouted. "Football, that's it."

"That's what?" asked Nick.

"Football, don't you get it?"

Nick didn't get it.

Jeremiah raced over to his computer. He worked three hours nonstop manipulating data and came up with the following:

More than 50 percent of the Democrats and only 10 percent of the Republicans are fans of the Minnesota Vikings while a resounding 80 percent of the Republicans and a mere 10 percent of the Democrats are fans of the Miami Dolphins; 80 percent of the Democrats watch the Super Bowl at a local bar with their drinking buddies while 90 percent of the Republicans watch it in a motel room with their mistresses; 40 percent of the Republicans played football for their college teams while none of the Democrats did.

Having established his argument, Jeremiah decided to develop it, and came up with the following:

More Republicans than Democrats were born in the month of January; Democrats, on the average, are an inch taller than Republicans; the average Republican is ten pounds heavier than the average Democrat and is likely to grow bald five years sooner.

Jeremiah could have gone on. He knew it. But he didn't need to. He had made his point and had made it well.

Just about everyone was dazzled by this latest performance. However, one person was actually nauseated and outraged. Her name is Sissy Black, and she is white.

Jeremiah was seated in his desk chair the morning after his "Is There a Difference?" story. It was the day before Christmas. There was a light coating of snow covering the streets. Leaning back, swiveling in one direction and then the other as he had seen Maynard do many times, he was gloating to himself about his success, humming out loud to the tune of "We Are Marching to Pretoria," every so often passing across the desk to Nick some scribbled quotes from admirers who had already gotten through to him on the phone.

He was thus engaged when Sissy marched straight up to where he was sitting and, with one hand on her hip and the other pointing in the direction of the door, growled, "Get out."

"What?" asked Jeremiah, startled and confused.

"I said" – she repeated slowly and deliberately – "get out."

"What do you mean?"

"I mean empty your desk drawer – " Sissy searched on top of the file cabinets and found some empty cartons and a D'Agostino shopping bag – "and get out."

"Are you out of your mind? What's got into you?"

"You have written your last piece of trash for this paper," she said.

"Trash? Do you know who reads this stuff?" asked Jeremiah, becoming heated. "Some of the most important, powerful, wealthy and self-serving people in this country. You should be praising me, not burying me. I have made you and your paper famous. I, myself, am being considered presidential material. Where's your gratitude?"

"Jeremiah, you're a slut," said Sissy, her voice sagging under the weight of her contempt.

"I'm angry with myself for ever believing in you," she continued. "I'm angry with myself for letting you besmirch the reputation of this paper by writing for it. I kept hoping you'd come around, do something worthwhile with yourself, stand up for something decent. Instead, you're like the rest, except you're worse, because you're better."

She walked over to the window.

"You tricked me," she said, sitting down on the windowsill. "I wanted to believe you were a man, or at least that you were struggling to become one. Instead, you're a pathetic little boy, dressed up in his football helmet and shoulder pads, except they don't fit. They were made for a ten-year-old. They look ridiculous. And you're so proud."

This was strong medicine. Jeremiah opened the top drawer of his desk and with his two hands swept up what he could gather and dropped it into a carton. When he had finished with that drawer he went on to the next. Sissy watched without saying anything. Nick felt he should say something but could really think of nothing.

"Sissy — " Nick said.

"Shut up," she said.

Meryl, who had been filing some papers, had overheard everything that was said. Before Jeremiah had packed his last pencil and paper clip everyone else in the office knew. They had gathered, quietly, two deep, in front of the row of desks near his cubicle, as they might have to watch a parade, catch a look at a visiting dignitary, a pedestrian who had just been hit by a car, or a casket being lowered into an open grave.

"Jeremiah," said Nick. "Wait. I'm coming with you." Nick grabbed a few things off his desk and followed Jeremiah out of the building into the blustery day.

CHAPTER 21

Same Day 2:30 P.M.

DESTINY PLAYS SUCH STRANGE tricks. Just when Jeremiah thought he had Her where he wanted Her, She had turned the tables on him. But the game wasn't over yet. Jeremiah had a few aces up his sleeve or, at least, thought he did.

Struggling down the narrow stairwell to the street with the remnants of his life's work in a few cartons and a D'Agostino shopping bag, he waxed philosophic about his fate.

"Here, give me the bag," said Nick.

"This is Destiny's handiwork," said Jeremiah. "She has a plan for me. Once She explains to me what She has in mind I'm sure I will be grateful."

"Jeremiah, watch where you're going," said Nick.

Nick and Jeremiah walked toward the corner of Avarice and Greed where there was a taxi stand and a waiting taxi. Nick ran ahead to get the taxi and turned back to watch Jeremiah casually walking into oncoming traffic, not taking the trouble to peer over the cartons he was carrying or look to see if any cars were coming.

Jeremiah was a little more than halfway across the street. Nick was signaling to the cab driver when he heard a woman scream out. He turned and saw a young woman standing with her child, waiting for a bus. She was pointing frantically in Jeremiah's direction. Nick looked behind him and saw a car heading straight for Jeremiah at full speed. Jeremiah dropped what he was carrying and took a fall backwards to get out of the way, and in the process put himself in the path of an oncoming truck. There was a screeching of brakes and an even louder, more piercing scream from the young woman at the bus stop.

"Jeremiah," Nick yelled.

Jeremiah lay on the ground, helplessly, as the cement mixer with its enormous tires headed straight for him, getting closer and closer, so close, no doubt, he could feel the heat of the engine, feel its rumble through the asphalt he was lying on. The truck came to a halt with one wheel touching his neck.

There was dead silence. No one moved. The door to the truck opened.

"You all right?" the burly looking truck driver asked, seeming a little put out by the turn of events.

"He's okay," said Nick, kneeling on the pavement next to his friend.

"He can't talk?" asked the driver.

"I think I'm okay," said Jeremiah, experiencing a sense of relief as a warm stream of urine spread across his pants and down his leg.

"That was the greatest micturition of my life," he said. "If I don't move I'll do just fine."

He was afraid that if he moved he would discover something about his body that he didn't want to know, or else that his body was serving as a wedge that was keeping the truck in place and that if he moved, it would role across his neck. The driver got into his truck, backed it up, pulled it alongside the curb, and came back to see what, if anything, had happened to Jeremiah.

103

"Can you get up?" he asked, giving Jeremiah two hands to grab on to.

Jeremiah rose to his feet, unsteadily at first, though nothing was wrong with him other than a bump on the back of his head.

The driver walked him to a bench in Hard Times Square.

"You with him?" he asked Nick.

"Yes," said Nick.

The driver went back to his truck, took something out of the glove compartment and returned with a scrap of paper with a telephone number and address and the name of his insurance company.

"If there are any problems, use this," he said.

"Thanks," said Nick.

"Nice guy," said Jeremiah, who seemed to be taking near-death in stride.

"Nice guy," Nick agreed.

"What was going through your mind?" asked Nick, "as you saw the tires getting closer and closer?"

"Well," began Jeremiah haltingly, for the first time feeling the shock of his ordeal, "I imagined I was living in a small town in Switzerland. It was wintertime and the streets were covered with snow. Horse-drawn sleds were the only means of transportation. I owned a small watch-and-clock repair shop on a narrow, winding street, in a building with its back to the Alps on one side, overlooking the valley below on the other, a valley which, in springtime, was a rich green, but which now, during the winter was laced with snow. I lived above the shop with my young daughter, Galinka, and my wife, who looked remarkably like Sissy Black, except her breasts had filled out, not to the size of Emma's at their peak, but to proportions of such sumptuousness that they provided a warm and comfortable resting place for my head during lunch hours, on those days when Galinka was at school, and at the end of a day's work, before blowing out the kerosene lamp at night, bringing another twenty-four-hour cycle of bliss to an end.

"I had Sissy on one arm and Galinka on the other. The three of us were about to begin the traditional Sunday afternoon rounds of the other villagers' homes, for the traditional grog and home-baked cakes, breads and cookies, along with hot chocolate and freshly brewed, aromatic teas, celebrating, in an abundance of warmth and kinship, the virtues of modest family living and an honest day's work, when I felt someone kicking at my foot."

"That was the truck driver," Nick concluded.

"That was the truck driver," agreed Jeremiah.

"That's what you were thinking as the cement truck rolled towards you?"

"That's what I was thinking."

As Nick and Jeremiah watched the truck driver cross the street, a strong gust of wind came along, lifting in a swirl much of the spilled contents of the cartons Jeremiah had been carrying. Hundreds of pages of text were carried into the air like so many stringless kites, spreading across the road, the sidewalk, the grass and trees of Hard Times Square, in an arc some thirty feet long. The young woman and her daughter tried to gather what they could and place it in one of the cartons that was still intact. Jeremiah waved them off. Another gust came and spread the sheets of paper even farther asunder, stories with such titles as, "War in the Middle East and the Sexual Response of the Average American Male," "Denial as a Way of Life," "Self-Immolation and the Role of Income Tax in American Culture."

One young man picked up a sheet of paper that came his way, read it quickly, made a face, and threw it in the waste basket along with a used Kleenex. One middle-aged woman, using her husband's arm for support, picked up a sheet of the paper and, without examining its contents, used it to wipe the dog droppings off the sole of her shoe. Jeremiah watched with detached bemusement.

Not bothering to look back and leaving behind whatever was retrievable of what he had once so highly prized, Jeremiah took the train back to New York.

CHAPTER 22

Same Day 4:30 P.M.

IT WAS LATE AFTERNOON by the time Nick and Jeremiah arrived at Jeremiah's place. On an ordinary day Jeremiah would have gotten home about six.

The apartment was quiet. No radio. No television. The table which might have been set for dinner was stacked with shopping bags filled with odds and ends collected off of end tables and shelves, which now lay bare.

Jeremiah called out to Emma. No answer. Nick followed him down the narrow hall to the bedroom. Emma was emptying the contents of one of her drawers into a suitcase.

"What's going on?" asked Jeremiah.

No response.

"What's going on?" he repeated.

Still no response.

Jeremiah grabbed her.

"What's going on?"

She shook herself free and gave Jeremiah a menacing glare. Jeremiah paused a moment to reflect.

"How did you know I was fired?" he asked.

"I called the office. Meryl told me everything."

"Did she tell you I was almost killed by a cement mixer."

"No, she didn't. Ask me if I care."

"And so that's it? After all we've been through."

"All we've been through? That's the problem. Your failure in business. This lousy, stinking, little apartment in one of the nastiness neighborhoods in town."

"What about the Watsons?"

"What about them? See if you can get Cawley on the phone once he learns what happened. Delusions, Jeremiah. Waiting on tables at Giacomos is where you belong. Maybe one day he would promote you to night manager. And what's more, Jeremiah, our sex life is a drag. I could have more fun with a bedpost."

"What!" said Jeremiah, for the first time painfully aware of Nick's presence.

The doorbell rang.

"Just a minute," yelled Emma.

"Do you know who that is?" she asked. "That is José."

Emma seemed to have developed a taste, some might call it a fetish or a compulsion, for Puerto Rican delivery boys. She had actually narrowed it down to D'Agostino delivery boys and would have none other. She would make her purchases, ask that they be delivered and then, as she was leaving, would survey who was working that day, make her choice and explain to the manager that she would prefer if José, Jesus or Juan made the delivery, since it was a particularly heavy load, slipping him ten dollars as she spoke.

José, Jesus, or Juan was more than eager to cooperate, no matter what the hour or what the load, because he knew that there would be an extra fifty dollars in it for him, once the job was done. Emma would greet her young man clad in a soft, sheer nightgown, retire to her room and wait for him to unpack the groceries. That was part of the arrangement. Then he would follow her to her room and slowly disrobe, singing as he did the words to "Celito Lindo." That was also part of the arrangement. And here was José standing at the door waiting to be let in.

Jeremiah turned red, and then white. He grabbed Emma's suitcase, threw it across the room and then went for Emma herself. Tripping across the wire to the cheap floor lamp that she had pulled in off the street one day, Jeremiah fell on his face. He rose to his feet and turned to confront his opponent, only to walk into the hard, cold barrel of the revolver her father had bought her the first time he had visited her Manhattan apartment.

The bell rang again.

Nick took a step towards Emma.

"Don't you move," said Emma, pointing the gun his way. "Get out," she said, directing the gun, first at Jeremiah then at Nick. "I'll be gone by seven."

Jeremiah hesitated.

"Let's go," said Nick, grabbing him by the arm.

CHAPTER 23

Christmas Eve 2003

JEREMIAH WAS SHAKEN. So was Nick. For Jeremiah to be free of Emma was a great gift. But for it to end this way, with a gun to his groin and a Puerto Rican delivery boy at the door, that was a bit much.

"We could go back to my place," said Nick.

"Nah," said Jeremiah, "let's go to Nika's."

Jeremiah led the way to a Greek luncheonette on lower Third Avenue, the kind of place where unshaven old men get a free cup of coffee and local workers on lunch break laugh too loud. Orders are yelled out across the counter to the short-order cook who is singing to himself in Greek. The phone rings nonstop for orders to go.

Watching Jeremiah dip his French fries into a pile of ketchup and then get his mouth around a cheap, undercooked hamburger oozing grease, Nick found himself wishing he were elsewhere.

"Delivery!" Nika yelled out. "Delivery!"

"You mean to say they actually deliver this stuff?" Nick asked.

"I gather the cuisine is not up to your standards," said Jeremiah, wounded by this cavalier reference to what he held to be sacrosanct.

"Don't get me wrong," said Nick, "I think this food," he simply could not control his sarcasm, "is really *interesting*."

Jeremiah was not to be easily appeased.

"Jeremiah," said Nick, once Nika was out of earshot, "don't be an ass."

"You don't get it," said Jeremiah, almost on the verge of tears.

"Get what?" said Nick. "That your balls were in a jar in the cabinet over the sink? That telling lies is one thing but that believing them is pretty goddamned fucked?"

Jeremiah stopped sniffling. A cloud of impotent rage crossed his face. With a sweep of his arm everything on the table went crashing to the floor. Every eye in the restaurant was on Jeremiah and Nick.

Nick got up and walked out.

Jeremiah sat motionless in the booth. Without disturbing him, Nika began cleaning up the mess on the floor. After about ten minutes of stupor, Jeremiah roused himself, left a $20 bill on the table and took the long way back to the apartment. It was a cold, crisp, windless evening. The streets were quiet. Everyone was inside celebrating Christmas. Jeremiah had about an hour and a half to kill befor Emma would be gone. He decided to take a bus uptown to look at the tree at Rockefeller Center. The bus was filled with families and tourists. The tree, dusted with snow, never looked so resplendent as it did on that particular day. There were people from everywhere, arm in arm, children in tow, young and old gathered around the ice-skating rink to watch the skaters. Never had Jeremiah felt more alone.

Around seven o'clock he returned home. The apartment was empty, just as Emma had said it would be. The bare rooms echoed with every move and footfall. The only noises he heard were the noises he made.

Jeremiah opened the refrigerator. Emma had cleaned it out.

There was a bottle of cognac on one of the open bookshelves. He poured himself a drink.

Seated in the rocker, Jeremiah could see through the now-curtainless window to the flashing neon sign across the street: "Checks Cashed." The room was lit with a red glow.

Jeremiah had lost his job, his wife, and almost his life, all in one day. Is this what Destiny had in mind? What could She possibly be thinking?

When Nick arrived the next morning, he found Jeremiah curled up on the couch facing the wall.

"Jeremiah, wake up," Nick said, shaking Jeremiah by the shoulder.

Jeremiah uncurled himself, turned around and opened his eyes. Pale and pasty, a crease across one cheek, a furrow between his eyes, lids swollen, hair a tangled mess, Jeremiah was not a pretty sight.

"You look like shit," Nick said.

Jeremiah looked at Nick without saying a word, seeming not to hear what he had said. Then all of a sudden he jumped out of bed and punched some numbers into the telephone.

"What are you doing?" Nick asked.

"Cawley Watson."

"Jeremiah," said Nick, "forget it."

It was 10:30, Thursday morning, Christmas day. Fong answered.

"Mr. Watson instructed me to tell you," said Fong in courteous tones, "that he is not available to speak with you and that he would not be in the future, due to a change in circumstances."

Jeremiah hung up the phone, slowly and deliberately.

"How the hell did he find out?" he asked in a soft monotone.

"Jeremiah, you have to get out of this place. There's an empty apartment in my building. I'll speak to the landlord on Monday. Come on, take a shower and we'll get some breakfast."

Jeremiah didn't move.

"Call me later," said Nick, halfway out the door.

111

CHAPTER 24

Later That Day

IT WASN'T UNTIL ABOUT one o'clock on Christmas day that Jeremiah began to stir. He took a long shower and began to think out rationally what had happened to him and what it all meant. He had almost been killed by a cement mixer. That was a bad thing. He was still alive. That was a good thing. He had lost his job. That was a bad thing. He had lost his wife. That was a good thing. He knew that all along but didn't want to admit it in front of Nick. Sure, he would be lonely at first. But he would get used to it. And already he was beginning to taste the freedom. As to his future employment, something would surely come up. It was just a question of time and patience. His needs were simple. He would accept Nick's offer and get himself a new place. That would be a fresh start.

As promised, after the New Year, Nick got Jeremiah an apartment in his building. Using his modest savings, Jeremiah set it up to suit his tastes and was pleased with the results. Two weeks into the new regime he had a new home. He was happier there than he had been anywhere in a long time. From his kitchen window, he looked down on 9th Street where he could see a stray dog pick at some garbage, a couple of East Village citizens propped up against a brick wall, wearing the filth they went to sleep in, a young mother with a tattoo and a ring through her nose pushing a stroller. This is city life as it should be, he thought, a heterogeneous tangle of misshapen souls all endowed with their inalienable rights and bad breath from cheap booze.

At first, Jeremiah was casual in his efforts to get another job. After all, he was Jeremiah Greenfield, probably the most celebrated journalist in the country. Soon it became apparent, however, that without a platform and an admiring public, he was just another unemployed reporter and that he would have to take what he could get. Then it became apparent that no one was going to hire someone with his name to do a routine job. And so he was frozen out at either end, with good jobs in the middle available only to insiders. Jeremiah was now on the outside. Gradually he began to accept the fact that there was no short-term solution to the unemployment situation and that he would have to find fulfillment in other ways. Sporadically he would return to the job hunt with renewed vigor and then pull back once again, thinking that it probably was the wrong season or the wrong opportunity or that maybe journalism wasn't what he really wanted anyway. At these moments, Jeremiah would become philosophical about life and realize that maybe it was time to focus on the here and now and experience the true richness of daily living.

After some adjustments and modifications, he gradually slipped into a routine – involving minimum expense and minimum effort – which he found not altogether unsatisfactory. He stopped shaving and getting haircuts, ate most of his food out of cans – it was cheap and there were no dishes to clean – took his daily shower and brushed his teeth. He would retire at around ten and get out of bed around noon.

He made a list of the television programs he wanted to watch — putting asterisks next to those which were of special interest — and began writing down his responses and critiques, thus investing this meaningless pastime with a degree of importance. In addition to television, there was breakfast, the plants to water, the garbage to put out, some errands to run and before he knew it, the six o'clock news, supper, the garbage to get ready for the next morning, and in no time it was bedtime.

Aside from a flat expanse in the middle, between noon when he got up and six when he had supper, a part of the day which is flat for most people whether they work or not, things really moved along quite swiftly and smoothly. The smallest of comforts began taking on the greatest of meaning. For example, Jeremiah bought himself some Polaner "Fancy Fruit Strawberry Preserves," which he would then spread over some fresh Keebler "Club Crackers." Seated by the window, watching the street life below, he would alternately nibble at the crackers and sip a cup of tea. The contrast between the sweet of the preserves and the salt of the crackers — its sharp bite in the back of the throat — the heat of the tea, the cool breeze from the partially opened window, all of these sensations Jeremiah eventually knew by heart. They filled him with a deep inner peace. And the combinations of sensations never failed. He could reproduce them at will and unlike making love, conversing with a friend, going to a movie or a concert, they never disappointed.

And there were other events, the routine of washing (there was no need to wash them, but that was the beauty of it) and lining up the empty cans of ravioli and arranging them in pairs along the counter under the cabinets, until there were exactly twelve, at which point Jeremiah would take them, one at a time, and toss them into a bag which he had placed against a door exactly eight feet from where he was in the kitchen — he had measured out the distance and etched a line into the linoleum floor — concentrating with great intensity as he made each toss and if he missed even one, starting all over until he reached a perfect twelve. What joy there was in that.

There were so many small comforts and small pleasures, each

pleasure different from the other, each pleasure with a size, a shape and a color of its own, like so many tiles in an intricately designed mosaic, embedded in the wall of some prehistoric cave whose meaning is truly known only to its creator. And who is to say that this life made up of these carefully crafted small comforts and pleasures is any worse, any less meaningful, any less desirable or worthwhile than that of the most successful banker, broker, businessman or butcher? Who is to say?

Jeremiah had other thoughts, thoughts of a darker nature. Briefly he would get a glimpse of the fact that he no longer had a life. At such moments it would strike him – from a purely philosophical point of view – that under the circumstances it made no sense at all for his biological existence to continue on. He had never considered death from this angle before but it occurred to him that in the ideal flow of things, quotidian and biological existence should draw to a close exactly at the same moment, like the simultaneous orgasms of two lovers, and that for biological existence to linger on once quotidian existence had drawn to a conclusion was a violation of some natural or aesthetic law. From a purely philosophical perspective, it made no sense whatsoever.

It was a pleasant day towards the beginning of April. Sunny thoughts had replaced the darker ones. Jeremiah had just spent some time sitting on a bench in Tompkins Square where he had actually made some acquaintances. Sure, he needed the month's rent. He would come up with it. He was feeling younger and freer that he ever had. It was as if he had discovered life for the first time, saw it for its true meaning and value. It had been there all along before him. He had been looking straight at it. But like an image hidden in a child's activity book – find the rake, the saw, the hammer, the duck – he had needed a slight change in perspective to make it visible.

He walked up the three flights of stairs, proud of the fact he was getting free of charge stair-walking exercise for which yuppies were spending three hundred dollars a month. The light in the hall was out. The first thing that caught his eye was the bag of groceries propped up against the wall. This was from Sissy.

When he got close enough to actually bend down and pick up the
bag of groceries, he saw that there was a notice of some kind affixed
to the door. He was ready to tear it off and throw it away, thinking
it was probably a menu from one of the Chinese restaurants.

As he moved towards the stairwell, where there was light coming from the skylight, he could see that what he had been about to
throw away was a printed notice from the housing court, a notice
making reference to previous notices issued from the same offices,
citing exact dates on which these previous notices had been issued,
explaining in stark prose, prose stentorian and unyielding, prose
admonishing and authoritarian, prose which had run out of patience
– for effect, underlining some words, putting others in caps – the
law, section and paragraph, filling in the blank where a name should
be with the name "Jeremiah Greenfield" and, in the next appropri-
ate blank, his address and apartment number, indicating that a
Spanish version was available upon request, informing "the occupant of said apartment" that, having exhausted "all available remedies," the landlord had repossessed "said premises" and that, in
essence, "said occupant" was out on his "said ass." That is what the
notice said, saying it as succinctly as it could, saying it thoroughly,
almost, but not quite repeating itself, so as to cover every conceiv-
able contingency and exception, tightening as it did, "said rope"
around "said occupant's" "said neck."

"Occupant Greenfield" had been in no uncertain terms evicted
from his apartment.

Naively believing that this was a paper notice only, Jeremiah
picked up the bag of groceries and, leaning against the door with
the weight of his body, reached into his pocket for the key, insert-
ed it as he usually did, turned it and pushed against the door to
open it. It seemed stuck. Then he put down the bag, turned the
key again, pulled up on the handle, as he had many times in the
past when the door wouldn't open, and pushing on the upper half
of the door made contact with a cold, heavy, metal object in the
shape of a padlock. Indeed it was a padlock and had been insert-
ed through a latch, one half of which had been secured to the door

frame, the other to the door itself, in effect, making it impossible to open the door, which is exactly why it was put there in the first place. Here was Destiny again, pulling a fast one on him. Had She no compassion whatsoever, no sensitivity, no mercy? Hadn't he been willing to settle for the humblest of existences if She would only leave him in peace? Hadn't he been a hard-working, rent-paying citizen for many years? Didn't She take these factors into account? Didn't She at least give some kind of warning or second chance?

Jeremiah pushed on the door again, this time harder. Then he yanked at the padlock, tugged at it with both hands, rammed his shoulder into the door, kicked the door, pulled at the handle of the door, shook it back and forth, kicked the door again and, "having exhausted" these "available remedies," began cursing. He cursed the door, the lock, the court, the law, the City of New York, the judge, the landlord, his mother, his father, an uncle of his he hadn't thought about for many years, and when he ran out of ideas, actually started cursing himself.

"You dumb stupid fuck. You dumb stupid fuck."

Jeremiah sank to the floor and actually wept.

If he could have died at that moment, he would have gladly, and with no regrets. If he could have willed his heart to stop beating, he would have so willed.

He held his breath as long as he could, hoping he would at least pass out. He didn't even get dizzy. Perhaps if he closed his eyes and fell asleep he would wake up to find that it had all been a bad dream. His eyes kept opening.

If he sat there long enough, maybe he would slip into a catatonic stupor. The landlord would come, see him slumped against the door. He would call the police. They would call an ambulance. Jeremiah would be transported to a hospital in upstate New York and housed in a rambling mental institution, free of care and responsibility. Early in the morning, before breakfast, he would take leisurely walks in the wooded area nearby, perhaps even teach some of the less fortunate to read, live to the ripe old age of eighty-nine, and then die a peaceful death in his sleep, fondly remembered by staff and patients in a moving memorial service in his honor.

But the catatonic stupor never came. In its stead, there was an ache in his back from sitting on the hard floor against the hard door.

Jeremiah walked up the two flights of stairs to Nick's apartment and knocked on the door, knowing full well he wasn't there. He would try again later.

CHAPTER 25

Same Day

FOR NOW JEREMIAH WOULD have to make do with the bag of groceries and a park bench. He walked down the stairs and out into the light of day. Once he was outside, it didn't all seem so bad. After all, there were other apartments in the City of New York and there were other cities, other states, other countries, other planets. There was a whole world to chose from. A whole universe. Why did it really matter that this one little, cramped apartment in a lousy neighborhood was being denied him? He would simply live somewhere else.

It was mid afternoon by the time Jeremiah made it to Tompkins Square with his bag of groceries. There was an empty bench. He sat down and placed the bag of groceries beside him. Without staring and without appearing to take notice, several homeless people acknowledged his presence, intuiting by the look in his face, his gait, his posture that, in fact, he wasn't there on his way home but that, in fact, he had no home. They just knew it and let him sit there for a while without bothering him.

A little boy approached Jeremiah's bench and without a hint of timidity stood in front of Jeremiah, staring.

"What's in the bag?" asked the boy.

"Cans. Food," Jeremiah said.

"I want some," said the boy.

Jeremiah reached in and held out a can of ravioli. The boy took it without a thank you and walked off in the direction of his family.

The breeze had calmed down a bit. Jeremiah closed his eyes and enjoyed the warmth of the sun. Here he was officially homeless by just about any definition and all but penniless and it didn't seem all that bad, certainly not as bad as he had thought. There was the peace that comes with knowing the worst and living through it.

After about half an hour of sitting on the bench, a rather unpleasant looking, ruddy-faced, unshaven, shabbily dressed man of no age in particular sat himself down beside Jeremiah and without so much as even a "nice day isn't it," looked into the bag of groceries – which clearly belonged to Jeremiah – and seeing what he wanted, reached in, took two cans and then walked off. Jeremiah watched as this was happening, thought of saying, "Hey, that's mine" or "What the fuck are you doing?" or "Do you mind?" but said nothing. He wasn't sure if it was out of fear or ignorance. Maybe the laws of property had changed. Maybe there were new etiquettes and protocols to learn. Maybe he was free to reach into someone else's bag of groceries just as this man had reached into his.

Seated on the ground across from him was a black man with a gray beard who had watched what had happened.

"They'll take the shirt off your back, if your let 'em," he said.

Now Jeremiah felt foolish. He had been conned. He had been willing to share the wealth and adjust to the new mores. But it turned out that the mores of the homeless weren't all that much different from those of the middle class. There was the same desperateness, the same possessiveness, but less verbiage in the execution. That was the chief difference.

These were Jeremiah's initial conclusions based on first impressions of homelessness. And as he was sitting on the bench being reflective about his new life, it suddenly dawned on him that he was living out a journalist's dream. Here he was in the middle of homelessness, not on its fringes, not pretending to be one of them just to gain their trust, but really one of them. Wasn't this a golden opportunity to get an insider's look at homelessness and then pass it along to his middle-class brothers and sisters, allow them to enjoy the romance of homelessness, provide them with an anthropologist's and a moralist's perspective after first filling them in with a lot of hard facts and some juicy anecdotal material?

There was at least one good article in homelessness, maybe a whole series — "Family Life of the Homeless," "Love Life of the Homeless," "Voting Patterns of the Homeless," "Property Rights Among the Homeless," "Twenty All Time Hits Chosen from Among a Random Sample of Twelve Hundred Homeless Men and Women Over Thirty" – the possibilities were endless. All Jeremiah needed was his laptop computer, which was locked in the apartment from which he had been evicted. That was an outrage. Homelessness was one thing. He was ready to cope with that. But no computer? That was unthinkable. Then it occurred to him that people had before – and some actually continued to – put pen to paper, which was better than nothing. Except he didn't have that either. He could buy some. Except that cost money and he had little of that to spare.

Then it came to him. Of course. All he had to do was ask, the way the young boy did, or take, the way the man did.

He got up from his bench and approached the black man with the gray beard.

"Got a pen and pad?" asked Jeremiah. "A pencil will do."

"Sorry," said the black man, shrugging his shoulders.

Jeremiah made his way from one cluster of people to the next, most of whom returned his query with a blank stare. One man held up a small stone and made a writing gesture. Jeremiah took the stone and started scratching into the black macadam of the path that wound through the square. That produced some legible results. But what would be the purpose of scratching his story into the ground if the goal was to send a story to the paper? Maybe he would invite Sissy to Tompkins Square to read and transcribe it? Maybe someone could come with a camera and photograph it? That was a real possibility. He would ask one of the tourists who came to inspect the homeless at Tompkins Square if he could borrow his camera to photograph what he had written. "Would you mind sending me the prints? I'm writing an important article on homelessness," he would say. But where would he have the prints sent?

For the first time Jeremiah realized that he had no address. That felt almost worse than being homeless and penniless. All of a sudden that junk mail and those bills seemed terribly important. They had supplied him with an identity. Each piece of mail addressed to him had confirmed the fact that he existed as a person. How, in fact, would the confirmation process take place if there were no receiving end, no destination for his mail to arrive at? He had no job. For all intents and purposes he had no friends. He had no home. What was he? Who was he? What was left of him? However, he had not yet been deported nor was he likely ever to be, which meant that at least he had a country. He was an American citizen. He had never before realized just how important that was to him, what a fine and upstanding thing it was just to be an American. He didn't have to earn a buck, own a car, or even have a roof over his head and he was still an American, was born one and would die one. That is who he was, an American, and damned proud.

"I'm an American," said Jeremiah aloud to no one in particular.

A couple of heads turned his way. Only the old black man seemed to understand.

"Good for you, brother," he said.

Jeremiah got up off the ground where he had started scratching his story into the macadam and walked over to the water fountain at the other end of the park to get a drink. He was surprised to find that the fountain actually worked. For sure, he wouldn't die of thirst. He returned to his spot on the bench. Curiously, it had not been taken. It was as if he had unknowingly staked a claim which the others were going to respect. He did have a place in the world after all. And the bag of groceries was just where he had left it.

He sat down, put his arm around the bag and drew it to him as one might a young child. The bag was quite a bit lighter than it had been when he brought it to the Square. In fact, he could tell, by its almost weightless quality, without even looking inside, that it was actually completely empty.

All of a sudden, though he had stuffed himself with pizza a little more than an hour ago, he felt pangs of hunger shoot through his stomach. He craved that food. It was his food, given to him by Sissy, and no one else had any right to it.

He looked around to see if he could tell who had taken the food. One person? Two? A whole family? Some lousy drunk son of a bitch or a mother and her toddler? Too bad for her if he found her. He would rip the food right out of her hands, or out of the hands of her starving child. He didn't give a damn. It was his. If he found it he was taking it.

Jeremiah started making the rounds. Staring into faces, daring them to defy him. Looking for the familiar cans. He would recognize them at once.

Then it occurred to him. The nice black man with the gray beard who had told him, "They'll take the shirt off your back if you let 'em," was gone. That lousy bastard. He was the one. He was just sitting there watching Jeremiah's every move, waiting for his opportunity. Didn't even take the bag. Why not? Was that part of the fun? Leaving the empty bag, setting him up to believe his food was in it and then laughing to himself imagining Jeremiah's surprise to find the bag empty. Lousy bastard.

By six-thirty Jeremiah was visited by real hunger pangs, not the sympathetic kind he had experienced after the black man had stolen his food. The true meaning of homelessness and hunger began to seep through. The romance had worn off. It had only taken an hour or so.

He would simply have to learn to live with hunger. It was just a question of an adjustment to be made, a new kind of conditioning. With time it would be no big deal at all. He would get used to it. This line of reasoning lasted for a half an hour, till about seven o'clock when Jeremiah became desperate, frantic and aggressively hungry.

"Hey, gimme a piece of that," he said to an old lady who was walking by with a baguette under her arm.

She tore off a piece. He didn't even say thank you.

One family, who were cooking some hot, gruel-like substance in a pot over an open fire, offered Jeremiah a portion. He accepted and ate he knew not what. At least his belly was full.

Jeremiah went back to his bench. It was getting dark, but he wasn't tired. There was no light to turn on. There was no television. He was afraid to leave his bench. If he lost that he would have to sleep on the ground. So he sat on the bench thinking about his predicament till almost midnight. Something would happen, surely it would. As a last resort, he could move in with his parents, a thought which, for some reason or other, had not occurred to him until that very moment.

Finally Jeremiah was getting sleepy. He hadn't dressed for the cool, night air. But there was a ready supply of cartons and plastic sheet scattered about the square. He got himself the cleanest cartons and plastic he could find, lay down on his bench, and pulled the dirty covering around him. He fell asleep quickly and slept through the night.

CHAPTER 26

Early May 2004

Anyone who had been keeping track of things at the *North Benware Star Ledger* would have known that, with Jeremiah gone, Nick was next in line for the job of editor-in-chief. He had been with the paper for more than ten years and could write. He had done some features and editorial pieces and knew his way around. So it was no surprise when, early in February, Sissy made an offer. Although it was presented as an offer, they both understood that if Nick didn't take it he would be advised to check out opportunities elsewhere and that if he did take it he would probably screw it up so badly that he would be asked to check out opportunities elsewhere. This was a fine example of what is known as "six of one and half dozen of the other." Nick chose six of one and decided to try his hand at the editorship.

He didn't have many friends at the *Ledger*. And for good reason.

Nick is the kind of person who borrows money and forgets to pay it back, the kind of person who is late for assignments. You can't do the story until he is there to shoot it. You get blamed for getting the story in late. Nick has irrefutable, carefully crafted excuses. With deliberation Nick does not sign the birthday card that is being circulated in your honor. But he drinks the beer and eats the pretzels at the party. So when word got around that he would be editor, there was a certain amount of good cheer in the office. Everyone was dying to see how long it would take him to fall on his face – there might actually have been some bets taken – and each in his or her small way would do what he or she could to see that it was sooner rather than later.

At first, Nick surprised everybody, especially himself. He took to the job and the routine. He understood exactly what Sissy wanted and had no problem delivering. She was really pleased. She actually gave him a big hug one day. He was getting a lot of respect and cooperation. It was as if he were a street orphan they had taken in, the scowling, dirty, mistrustful little kid who, with a shower, a new set of clothes and some food in his belly, actually turns out to be a person. Everyone wants to see him succeed. And that's just what Nick was doing.

Except after a month, Nick started coming in late in the morning, took longer and longer liquid lunches, called meetings and then forgot to attend. Surprisingly, people covered for him and made excuses. Then it almost became a tug of war. Nick had to come in even later and take even longer lunches and miss even more meetings until they would finally accept the fact that he was a screw-up. By the time May rolled around, everyone was convinced. Soon he would be shown the door, just as Jeremiah had been. Then he had an idea. Presidential politics were starting to heat up. Just suppose that Jeremiah had been approached by some backers. Wouldn't wavy-haired Bob want to know and wouldn't there be a buck in it for Nick? Nick decided to give him call.

"Mr. Shoreham's office," the secretary answered.

"This is Nick Belladonna."

"Just a minute, please."

"Nick, is that you?" asked Bob in his friendliest twang. "I can't believe it. Just this morning I told my secretary to get a hold of you. We have a proposition for you. Why don't you hop on a plane?"

"Sure," said Nick, haltingly, unprepared to have his wishes anticipated.

"Great," said Bob, "see you soon."

On the following day Nick found his way to the address on Q Street that Bob had given him. He was shown into an office where there was a big slab of a mahogany desk on a raised platform, mahogany shelves lined with trophies, memorabilia and autographed photos. To the right of the desk and behind Bob was a flagpole with the American flag at full mast. Nick couldn't take his eyes off the flag.

Without getting up, Bob extended his hand for Nick to shake, noticing his fascination with the flag.

"That's a reminder," said Bob, "of how I got where I am. I want to be sure that I never forget that I owe her everything. Because without her...well, without her, I probably would have ended up like some of my less fortunate countrymen," he said with a barely suppressed smile and a knowing look in his eyes.

Sensing he might have crossed a line, Bob shifted gears pretty quickly. He reached down beside him, picked up an attaché case, set it on his desk and opened it up for Nick to see.

"As I'm sure you're aware," said Bob, "the president is not doing so well. We at CRAP feel that it would be a great loss for America if he didn't win the next election. We want to do everything we can to make sure that he has the opportunity to continue with the fine job he has been doing. Which is why you are here. Your friend Jeremiah is just what we are looking for. We want someone with an image and some notoriety to get out there, mount a campaign and siphon off enough votes from the Democrats to give our man an easy victory."

"So you want Jeremiah to get in the ring for a couple of rounds and then take a fall."

"Exactly," said Bob. "I knew you would understand. Jeremiah will be heading up a third party, known as PISS or the Party to Insure Safety and Security. His campaign will be geared to the average middle-class American's fear for his life. You will have the best in staff and PR firms at your disposal and whatever funding you need."

Bob opened a desk drawer and pulled out a prospectus of the apartment building on 57th Street where Jeremiah and Nick would be living. There was a layout of the fifteen-room penthouse apartment and a photograph of the view from the thirty-foot, wrap-around terrace. There would be a full-time cook, a cleaning service, a $10,000 clothes allowance, a $200,000 bank account, $30 million worth of campaign funds and an unlimited supply of freshly laundered cloth napkins.

Bob opened up another drawer and came up with a set of keys.

"This one is for the apartment," he said. "And this one is for the Ferrari."

He nudged the keys across the desk in Nick's direction.

Saying nothing, Nick nodded his head in agreement, picked up the keys and attaché case and took the next plane back to New York. He should have been thrilled, but wasn't. Something had changed. But he really had no choice. So, for the time being, Nick would have to make do with the Ferrari and the apartment on 57th Street. Sissy would be grateful that he had relieved her of the burden of firing him.

CHAPTER 27

Later That Afternoon

IT WAS POURING WHEN Nick landed at LaGuardia. There was a long line for taxis. He finally got one and gave the driver the 57th Street address. The building Bob had chosen was a glass-slab high-rise not far from Carnegie Hall, with a slick lobby and officious staff. Nothing about the building was real. Nick was ushered to the door of the apartment by the elevator operator, who insisted on taking the key from him and opening the door.

Nick closed the door behind him and out of habit double-locked it. He stood in the entryway and surveyed the apartment, which was right off the cover of *Architectural Digest*. Everything was in white, beige and gray, with a few touches of color in the pillows. There were glass tables and mirrors everywhere, elaborate built-in cabinets, shelves and closets, some interesting abstract prints on the walls and impressive potted plants. The apartment was at once simple, elegant, dazzling and lacking in warmth. It would take some getting used to.

Nick walked over to the long modular seating area, sat down, took one of the pillows and threw it halfway across the room, watching it come to a rest in the soft gray carpeting. Perhaps if he messed things up a bit he would feel more at home.

In the kitchen, there was a broad expanse of windows, a center island for prep work, lacquered cabinets, recessed lighting, and two double sinks with hardware that glistened. There was some soda in the refrigerator and a well-stocked liquor cabinet. There were towels in the linen closet and not much more. Someone would have to do some shopping.

The next day Nick gave Sissy two weeks notice. It was fine with her if he left that afternoon, she explained. She would be more than happy to pay him two weeks salary. Nick thanked her for her generosity and immediately called Bob. Bob was very pleased and told Nick that staff would be in place by Friday. Nick spent the next few days lolling about the apartment, listening to music and exploring the neighborhood.

At ten o'clock on Friday morning, the doorbell rang. Nick opened the door cautiously and studied the person behind it.

"Hello," she said, extending her hand. "I'm Meghan."

"Hello," said Nick.

Meghan rested her leather briefcase on one of the glass coffee tables in the living room and opened it up. She took out a few labeled folders and a yellow lined pad and was ready to get down to business.

"You're not Jeremiah Greenfield," she said.

"No," said Nick.

She seemed confused.

"Who are you?"

"I'm Nick."

"No one told me about a Nick."

"I'm Jeremiah's campaign manager."

"I didn't know he had one."

"He does. And I'm it."

Things were coming out harsh and unfriendly. That isn't the way Nick wanted it.

"How about a drink?" he said.

"That would be nice," said Meghan.

He handed her a can of soda and all of a sudden realized that he had yet to call Jeremiah and tell him the news. Rather bizarre, he thought. Everything in place but the candidate himself.

"Excuse me," Nick said to Meghan. He went into the bedroom and closed the door.

Nick felt uncomfortable calling Jeremiah. There had been hard feelings once Jeremiah had lost the editorship and Nick had taken it on. At first, after Jeremiah was fired, Nick stopped by on a regular basis and tried helping Jeremiah get back on his feet. Soon he grew impatient with Jeremiah's self-pity and passivity. Though only two flights of stairs separated them, it had been a month or so since they had had any contact.

Nick called Jeremiah's apartment and got a recording saying that Jeremiah's service had been disconnected. Then he called the *Ledger* and learned from Sissy that Jeremiah had moved back in with his parents in upstate New York. She gave Nick the phone number.

"Hello, Jeremiah? It's Nick."

"Hi," said Jeremiah, clearly taken off guard.

"How are you?" Nick asked.

"Nick, why are you calling?"

"Jeremiah, you're so cynical. I'm calling out of friendship. Why else would I call?"

"Because you want something, or because you have a used car to sell," said Jeremiah.

"You're getting close. Actually, I do have a used car to sell. And I think you are going to want to drive this one off the lot. How would you like to fulfill your lifetime ambition and run for the president of the United States?"

No response. For sure Jeremiah didn't believe Nick and even if he did, Nick had the feeling that his attitude had changed quite a bit over the past year. This was going to be a hard sell.

"Jeremiah. I'm on the level. I'm calling from a magnificent apartment on 57th Street. $30 million in funding, $200,000 expense account, the works."

"Nick, you can keep the apartment and the money."

"No, I understand," said Nick, backtracking. "No, it's not about the money. It's about being president. What you've always wanted."

"Who's behind it?"

"CRAP."

"And what do they want from me?"

"PISS. They want you to head up the Party to Insure Safety and Security".

"What do I owe them if I get elected?"

"Who said anything about owing anyone anything?"

"Nick, don't bullshit me."

"It'll all be worked out. Don't worry about it."

Of course, Nick wasn't saying everything. There was the part about Jeremiah's taking a fall. He figured Jeremiah would have some fun and probably couldn't win anyway. So why burden him with unnecessary details?

"I tell you what," said Nick, "why don't you get on a train. We'll talk about it. You'll meet Meghan. At least you will see that I am not making it up."

"Who is Meghan?"

"She's your press secretary and administrative assistant. I think you'll like her."

"Okay," he said solemnly. "What's the address?"

Nick gave him the address and hung up.

Things weren't working out the way he had hoped. Nick had lost his enthusiasm. Jeremiah had lost his. Even Meghan seemed hesitant and suspicious. Why were they doing this?

Nick found Meghan where he had left her, scribbling away on her yellow lined pad.

"I just spoke to Jeremiah. He'll be here in a couple of hours."

Meghan looked up, sensing that something was out of kilter, but didn't say anything.

"What's Jeremiah like?" she asked. "I've heard a lot about him. But I've never met him."

"I think you'll like him," said Nick. "He's easy-going. He's a good writer, a good speaker. He can rise to the occasion."

"What about CRAP? Who are they? I got this job through an agency."

"The less you know about CRAP the better. I don't know a lot and that's already too much."

The bell rang. Nick opened the door. There was a short, dark-haired woman holding a couple of bags of groceries.

"I Sala," (i.e., Sarah) she said in a clipped Oriental accent.

"Hello, Sarah," Nick said, taking the bags.

"No," she said. "I take."

Sarah bustled past Nick and began preparing the evening meal.

About seven-thirty, the bell rang again. This time it was Jeremiah.

"So this is it," he said, standing in the entranceway not knowing what to do with himself.

"This is Meghan," said Nick.

Meghan took his hand and smiled warmly. Jeremiah stared at her intently, as if he had met her once before and was trying to remember when.

"Well," said Nick nervously, "why don't you take a look around?"

Jeremiah began inspecting the furniture as if he were about to buy it. Stood in front of the wall hangings, studied them, but said nothing.

"Come on," said Nick, putting his arm around his friend's shoulder. "This is going to be fun. I'll tell you what. Suppose we buy back the lease to your apartment and help you get set up. We have plenty of money. It will be like a satellite headquarters. You can stay there for the time being."

The offer seemed to lift Jeremiah's spirits. Nick decided to take a walk before dinner, giving Jeremiah some time to get used to the apartment and to get to know Meghan.

Jeremiah watched Meghan as she went through some papers and began taking notes. Stark white skin, auburn hair pulled back in a bun. There was something about her. He caught a glimpse of a framed photo.

"Do you mind?" he said, pointing to the photo.

"No. That's my daughter Kelly."

Returning his gaze was a young girl about seven years old with auburn hair like her mother. Her head was tilted to one side as if to say, "What do you think?" There was a dimple in her cheek and sadness in her eyes.

"She's pretty," said Jeremiah, carefully replacing the photograph.

"Her father was shot dead in Dublin," she said, almost matter-of-factly.

"Dooblin," she said. It was like listening to poetry to hear her speak.

Watching her as she drank her soda, Jeremiah realized that Meghan lived in a world that he could never penetrate, a world of nobility, fierce pride and fearlessness where the creature comforts that Americans so prized had little meaning. He momentarily wished he could escape into such a world and be cleansed.

"I don't think there is anything I would willingly give my life for," he said.

"You are right," she said. "A man dies. Nothing changes."

"I would like to want to die for something," said Jeremiah, uttering a thought he had never before had.

"You are a romantic, you know. Are you sure you're not Irish?"

Jeremiah picked up Kelly's picture for a second look. Those eyes. That sadness, the auburn hair. Then he made the connection. He was seeing those saddened eyes through the screen door that day in August, twenty-one years ago. He studied Meghan more carefully and imagined her as Katelyn full grown. They had the same skin, the same color hair. Katelyn was shorter. Her eyes a different color. It was not the same mouth. But when he stood back and squinted his eyes, Jeremiah could see Katelyn seated at the coffee table. Meghan sensed his eyes upon her.

Nick returned from his walk.

"Dinner leady," piped in Sarah.

Dinner, indeed, was ready. Sarah had set a beautiful table. There was an open bottle of white wine in a cooler, a simple flower arrangement in the middle of the table and the first course in place: green-colored, cold spring rolls cut on the bias and standing upright, stuffed with asparagus, scallions and smoked salmon, in a yellow pepper coulis.

Nick poured out three glasses of wine and proposed a toast.

"To the next president of the United States."

It seemed so incredibly preposterous. No one said a word. Then they all burst out laughing at once, "To the next president of the United States."

The three of them had a most enjoyable meal, talking small talk and nonsense for almost two hours. Nick suggested they wait till the morning before getting down to business. There were no dissenting opinions.

CHAPTER 2 8

The Next Morning

EARLY THE NEXT MORNING, Jeremiah, Nick and Meghan were looking over piles of newspaper clippings that were spread across the dining room table. This was material gathered by Meghan on the front-running Democratic candidate, Milton Kindly.

The Democrats, in a shrewd strategic move, decided to go for the "Gray Vote" and, in an unusual show of unity, threw all their support behind a 75-year-old retired school teacher. The ploy worked. Early polls showed that 95 percent of the near-dead supported "Milt" Kindly for president.

Milt, who had considerable short-term memory loss, spoke in a stutter about vague and unrepeatable plans he had for making America a "decent country to die in." He uttered simple homilies in a way that was reassuring and comforting, and reminisced about his first job as a soda jerk at the age of sixteen, and how he used the money he earned to help his father go into business as a zipper sales-man, frequently losing track of his subject matter midsentence. Jeremiah recognized that Milt would not be an easy target.

At about eleven o'clock Meghan ushered in a thin, tall man, with a little boy's face and a shock of black hair across his forehead, dressed in a dark blue, pin-striped suit in the latest Italianate style, sporting red suspenders.

"This is Frank Treason," said Meghan.

Frank was a corporate attorney from "Steel Balls of America," a manufacturer of lead weights for fishing tackle, with a background in public relations who was on loan to Jeremiah's campaign. He declined the offer of Jeremiah's extended hand and instead picked some peanuts out of the small bowl on the coffee table. Sitting him-self down, he rested his outstretched arms across the edge of the couch in a gesture of freedom and arrogance.

"So you're Jeremiah Greenfield," he said, looking around the room as he spoke. "Nice digs." Then he slumped down in his seat and extended his long frame, resting his feet on the coffee table and his hands behind his head.

"This is a one-issue campaign, Jerry. Safety and security," he said. "Your mascot is a pit bull terrier named Stanley. You and Stanley will be together all the time, on posters, on TV. There will be footage of you walking Stanley down the street at night and of him scaring off would-be attackers and insurance salesmen."

Treason leaned forward and took a few more peanuts.

"You are tough, Jerry, damned tough and that's going to come through. You will be seen lifting weights, practicing karate and dragging homeless men out of doorways."

He dropped his legs to the floor and sat forward in his seat.

"You don't know anything about foreign policy. You don't know anything about taxes, education, conservation. You are an expert on door locks of every kind, prisons, hidden camera security, police tactics, riot control, purse snatching and petty theft. Your running mate is a nice guy. I think you'll like him. Lyndon Boyle. He's a retired detective."

Then he stopped short.

"Any questions?"

"None," said Jeremiah somberly.

"We get going seriously on Monday. You'll have a wardrobe advisor, a hair stylist. We'll get you into the studio on Tuesday, which is where you'll spend the rest of the week. In two weeks we'll have the posters and buttons rolling, and more film footage than we know what to do with. The PISS party is on the ballot in all fifty states. On Friday, June fourth, you are going to have your first news conference, announcing your candidacy for president as a third party candidate. I'll be writing the speeches. You'll be mouthing them." With that, Treason excused himself, helped himself to a beer from the refrigerator and was gone.

Jeremiah, Nick and Meghan were left mute. Meghan was biting her lip. Jeremiah was working his jaw.

"Let's get out of here," Nick said. "There's a place to get some lunch on the corner."

They spent the rest of the day being busy about nothing.

The June fourth news conference was held as planned with the prison on Riker's Island as a backdrop.

"On the way over here," began Jeremiah before a bank of cameras and microphones, in a casual, folksy way, "I saw a young black man push an old white lady out of the way as she was getting on the subway. That should not be allowed to happen in this free, peace-loving country of ours. That's why we have buildings like this," he said, pointing behind him, "and that's where men like that belong.

"Old white ladies should be free to roam this land at will," he continued, "frustrating the hell out of all of us as they fumble through their change purses at the checkout counter. That is what democracy is all about.

"I know what some of you are thinking, 'Oh, here's another safety and security act.' Well this isn't just another safety and security act," said Jeremiah, doing a rapid, turning karate kick and knocking a microphone out of the hand of one of the reporters. "This is safety and security that means business." The cameras caught a shot of Stanley, Jeremiah's pit bull mascot, with one of the reporters' legs clamped in his jaw.

Jeremiah paused to consult his notes.

"I have been listening to Mr. Kindly's speeches. I've heard what he has to say on dentures and prostheses. But what about safety and security, Mr. Kindly?"

Here Jeremiah paused for effect.

"My friends," he said, casting his eyes across the group of reporters hanging on his every word, "it's time for a change. It's time for action. We're tired of being mugged, raped and robbed and I have developed a four-point program to set things in the right direction."

Jeremiah searched his papers for the document in question, which he then read at a slow and deliberate pace, accenting each of the four points with an index finger in the air.

"One. Buy the best locks money can buy. Two. Never park your car on the street. Three. Never stay out after nine in the evening. Four. Always look behind you when walking home at night."

This caused quite a stir. Several reporters jumped up from their seats, shouting questions.

"Which locks are the best?" asked one nervous young woman. "I never know which to buy."

"What about garages? We're running out of space. What are you going to do about that?" asked another reporter in an angry tone.

Ignoring the questions, Jeremiah ceremoniously closed the folio of papers he had been working from and then smiled.

"Thank you," he said, looking into the camera for a long meaningful moment before it switched to the TV reporter who summed up what had just happened and then broke for a laxative commercial.

Frank Treason, who had been intently watching Jeremiah's performance, broke into a broad grin.

"Nice work," he said.

The four of them, Frank, Jeremiah, Nick and Meghan, rode back to the city in a limousine. Frank got out at 42nd Street, Nick in front of Barney's on Madison Avenue. That left Meghan and Jeremiah.

"Why don't we go to Yonkers instead of that fish bowl you call home?" she said. "You can meet my mother and Kelly."

"Why not?" said Jeremiah.

CHAPTER 29

Later That Day

MEGHAN LIVED IN A three-story, cedar shingle row house built at a time when the lower middle class could still afford decent housing. It was a solid but uninspiring structure with an inviting front porch. There was a small plot of grass in the front and a slightly more substantial backyard, shaded by large apple tree from which Mother O'Toole gathered apples for her apple pies and cakes.

Mother O'Toole was – like the house she lived in – solidly built, a large-boned woman with white skin and orange-colored hair turning white. She wore thick lenses and spoke with a heavy brogue.

"Why don't ye go on into the kitchen now," she said, addressing her daughter while taking Jeremiah's measure, "an' start peelin' potatoes far dinner while Mr. Greenfield and I, we have us a friendly little chat."

Meghan did as she was told.

Mother O'Toole held the door open. Jeremiah took the hint and led the way out on to the front porch where there were two comfortable-looking rockers.

They rocked in silence. After exchanging pleasantries about the weather, life in the city, the campaign, Mother O'Toole got right to the point.

"Yeer the shiftless kind now, aren't ye, Mr. Greenfield?" she said, not looking his way.

Jeremiah said nothing. Mother O'Toole reflected some more and then continued.

"Yeer a liar, now aren't ye, Mr. Greenfield. And a damned good one, I bet," she said almost admiringly. "I've known some liars in my time. I was married to one. I want better for Meghan."

Jeremiah stiffened in his chair and took a sidewise glance at the woman sitting next to him.

"To begin with," said Jeremiah, "though I do lie from time to time – it is what I do for a living – I would never do anything to harm Meghan."

"Mr. Greenfield," continued Mother O'Toole, ignoring everything Jeremiah had said, "yee are the worst kind of liar of all, the one who lies to himself."

"What are you talking about?" he said, his voice rising. "You don't even know me."

Jeremiah got up from the rocker and walked down the porch steps.

"I know ye better than ye know yeerself. Lies, Mr. Greenfield," she said, leaning over the railing and speaking more forcefully. "Lies fallin' like snowflakes. No two alike, but they are really the same. And what will they get ya that's worth havin', now? Not mooch, Mr. Greenfield. Not mooch. The warld don't need no more liars, ya know. What we'll be a needin' is a little truth."

Mother O'Toole got up from her chair, opened the screen door to the house, then paused and turned.

"Heed me warnin', Mr. Greenfield," she said, her voice quivering slightly. "Liars die a cruel death."

A yellow school bus pulled up in front of the house, its lights flashing. The door opened and a young girl with auburn hair jumped to the ground.

"Don't jump," yelled Mother O'Toole.

The little girl smiled, swung her book bag back and forth, and took a zigzag path across the grass, watching her shadow as she walked. Looking sideways at Jeremiah, she kissed her grandmother on the cheek.

"This is Mr. Greenfield," said Mother O'Toole.

Kelly studied Jeremiah as she might a caged puppy in a pet shop, deciding if this was the one she wanted or not.

She shrugged her shoulders as if to say, "He'll do," and then headed up to her room.

Jeremiah and the O'Tooles sat down to a meal of boiled beef, boiled potatoes and raw vegetables.

"We eat simple food," said Mother O'Toole, as if reading Jeremiah's mind.

The evening passed pleasantly with Kelly leading the conservation until it was time for her to go to bed. Mother O'Toole excused herself. Meghan and Jeremiah went out on the front porch and sat down. It was a starry, moonless night.

"Don't mind my mother," said Meghan, sensing that something had gone awry. "She speaks her mind but she means no one ill. She will be your loyal friend if you let her."

"She crucified me. Why would she want to be my friend?"

"That is her way," said Meghan.

Jeremiah felt heavy with sadness. But wasn't Mother O'Toole merely repeating aloud what he had said to himself many times before? Weren't her words an echo of the thoughts he had that day, seated on the bench in Hard Times Square, feeling so low that even being accepted by homeless man was too much for him to expect? And here he was in the middle of a political campaign spouting one lie after another. How did he get so far off track again? Wouldn't life be so much simpler and freer if he just spoke the truth?

"You are running, Jeremiah," Meghan continued.

"Not you, too. I didn't come up here to have my soul saved."

"Maybe you did and don't know it."

Jeremiah sat back in his chair and closed his eyes for a moment.

"I admit it, this campaign business was a big mistake," he said by way of a confession. "It is not what I really want anymore. It feels as if it is going to suck us all in and that there is nothing we can do to stop it."

"It can be a good thing or a bad thing, Jeremiah. That depends on you."

Pause.

"I can see the Big Dipper," she said.

He looked up.

"No," she said, taking his hand and pointing it to the left. "Over there."

"Very nice," he said.

"You didn't really see it," she said, getting out of her chair. "See it? It's right there."

Jeremiah got up out of his seat and leaned over the edge of the railing. He could feel Meghan's body next to his. He looked up into the night. For a moment nothing else mattered but the darkness, the sparkling white light and Meghan beside him.

CHAPTER 30

The Last of July 2004

THE CAMPAIGN GOT OFF to a good start and did better and better
with the passing of each day. Jeremiah and Meghan were con-
stantly together. As his schedule would allow, he spent time in
Yonkers. Meghan was right, Mother O'Toole had said what was on
her mind and from that day forward treated Jeremiah with kind-
ness, almost as if he were one of the family. Jeremiah wished more
and more that he were. Everything he wanted from his childhood
and didn't get he could have gotten if this had been his home.

Meghan took to helping Jeremiah with his wardrobe, purchased
shirts and ties for him, was there to remind him of his appointments
and encourage him at difficult moments. They were brought closer
and closer together. His birthday was in a week. The campaign was
starting to wear him down.

"Suppose we get away," he said as they got out of a cab on 57th

Street. "Just the two of us for the weekend. I promise to behave."

Meghan stood still. She didn't say no. She didn't say yes.

"Separate beds," she said.

"Separate beds," he said.

"Maybe a spot by the sea. The Massachusetts coast?" she asked.

"Yes," he said.

Jeremiah made it to Yonkers by eight the next morning. They stopped for breakfast at a local diner and were halfway to the coast by eleven. They got off the turnpike at Lee. The foliage was lush. The back roads were deserted. Life seemed simpler and less menacing.

They spent one night in a large, rambling inn and had blueberry pancakes and homemade sausage for breakfast. By midafternoon of the second day they had reached a small fishing village on the coast.

Windward-by-the-Sea, once a center for whaling, then an active fishing port, then one of the largest producers of lobsters in the country, hung on to the land like a caterpillar to a fallen leaf. The town jutted out into the ocean on any available spit of land, nestling into harbors both natural and man-made.

They walked along a narrow street lined with tightly packed, small, weathered buildings that were fishermen's shacks going back a hundred years or more, presently housing souvenir, candy, T-shirt and schlock art shops for nondiscriminating day-trippers from Boston.

They enjoyed homemade strüdel and freshly steamed lobsters, which they ate *al fresco* off crates on an open deck, overlooking the harbor. Sailboats tugged at their moorings and ropes clanked against their masts like wind chimes.

"It's so peaceful here," said Meghan as they sipped hot chocolate. "It doesn't seem real. But it is. These people have lives. Can they be miserable in such a beautiful setting?"

"Human beings are ingenious creatures," Jeremiah replied, toying with a wooden stirrer. "They've probably found a way."

They took a two-mile ride down a winding country road and picked a restaurant on the water that was loud and raucous. Rawskinned, bearded locals in fisherman's boots were drinking beer by the mug and singing along with the piano. There were couples and even some families with young children seated at small tables with checkered tablecloths.

Jeremiah ordered two beers. Meghan raised her mug and began singing along to "When Irish Eyes Are Smiling." She moved the mug in time with the music, splashed some beer on her face and began laughing. With that simple expression of joy, Jeremiah saw everything that was missing in his life and everything that he wanted.

"I love you," he said through the clamor.

Meghan leaned across the table and kissed him. The couple got up and started dancing to "Sweet Adeline." They ate the contest-winning clam chowder, had fried clams and key lime pie and ended the evening with a rousing chorus of "We Ain't Got a Barrel of Money" sung in harmony.

On the street, in front of the pub, Jeremiah took Meghan in his arms and held her tightly. He drove back to the inn, one hand holding hers. They made love and fell asleep in each other's arms.

CHAPTER 31

September 2004

Winning Meghan was becoming more important than winning the election. Nonetheless, after three months of hard work, Jeremiah had made a significant dent in his opponent's rating. Soon he was taking points from the incumbent. That was not the way it was supposed to be.

By mid-September, Jeremiah had 35 percent of the projected vote, Milt Kindly had 25 percent and the incumbent 40 percent. This was a dangerous state of affairs. Frank told Nick to get Jeremiah to pull back and let things settle a bit. Even so, by late September, Jeremiah and the incumbent were almost even at about 40 percent apiece, and Milt, who had become incontinent and was forgetting his campaign appearances altogether, made the only intelligent choice and actually dropped out. In addition to his stutter, he had now developed a slur. It was almost impossible to understand him.

His announcement was both shocking and pathetic. Milt spoke very slowly, struggling with each syllable.

"Ladies and g-g-gentlemeth," he began, "I have decithith thou whiraw fr-fr-from thuh campine." This stunned everyone. Then Milt went on to praise Jeremiah and explained that he was throwing his full support behind him, encouraging everyone else to do likewise. Frank Treason's jaw dropped. Meghan just shook her head.

"Look," said Frank nervously when Nick and he were alone, "I don't know what this means. This might be made to order if we play our cards right. Now we have complete control over the numbers. It's a narrow line to walk. Jeremiah has to fight the fight to make it credible while setting himself up for the knock-out punch. Don't do anything until you hear from me. I have to speak to CRAP."

A few days later, Treason and Nick met at a bar on Broadway. The word from CRAP was to lay low. They needed time to come up with some new ideas.

"Jeremiah," Nick said, "I've been speaking to Mr. Treason. He feels that in order to hold on to what we have we should slow down a bit. He's afraid that if we run full out right now we won't have enough to finish the race with. He suggested you can your appearances for the next week until we have time to regroup."

"I don't know," Jeremiah said. "We're on a roll. I think we can overtake him by such a distance that he'll never come back."

"You might be right," Nick said, starting to get nervous himself. "But on the other hand, Mr. Treason and his friends have control of the money."

"Well," said Jeremiah, reluctantly. "I suppose we could pull back for a week."

The following Tuesday, Nick got a call from Treason. There was to be a meeting at a new restaurant that had opened on Third Avenue in the eighties, featuring pig meat in all of its forms. Waitresses had little corkscrew tails attached to their rear ends. Prices were listed as "oinks." Frank ate lustily.

"Jeremiah," he said, his lips moist with pig fat, "CRAP is pleased with what you've accomplished, very pleased. No one had expected it would work this well. In fact, it might have worked too well. I think CRAP underestimated your potential as a candidate. They think you have a much better chance as an underdog than as a clear winner. They want you to continue to be visible, but they want you to change your strategy. From now on, you're going to speak the truth."

Tell the truth. Everyone thought that was very funny, especially Jeremiah.

"Why not talk about yourself," advised Treason. "That's a good starting point."

At first, Jeremiah had no luck at all. The lies just kept multiplying themselves. Each lie was followed with a broad smile. To a group of Long Island potato farmers who had been forced to sell out to a consortium of Japanese and Canadian real estate developers, he said, "American farmers have never had it better." To a rally of local residents in Mahwah, New Jersey, in the parking lot of a Japanese electronics company that had once been the site of a Ford assembly plant, he said, "The American worker has never had it so good." To a group of meat packers in Chicago he asserted, "Statistics have shown, beyond any reasonable doubt, that the meat-packing industry is one of the safest in the country." Jeremiah had to be escorted to his car by security guards. How would he ever learn to speak the truth? Jeremiah decided it was time to pay Dr. Nostrum another visit.

"So you've decided you want to speak the truth," said Nostrum, leaning back in his chair, bouncing one thumb off the other.

"Yes," said Jeremiah.

"What has made you change your mind? The lies seem to be working just fine."

"There has been a change in strategy. I'm not supposed to lie anymore."

"Jeremiah, it is not possible to change one's character simply as a matter of expediency. To change in a fundamental way you need powerful motivation. Telling the truth has to mean more than getting a few votes."

Jeremiah reflected.

"I really don't like myself the way I am," he said. "I never have. I would like to be worthy of someone like Meghan."

"Who is Meghan?"

Jeremiah explained.

"You have to do this for yourself, Jeremiah. Not to win Meghan's favor."

Jeremiah thought some more.

"The truth will set us free. I know that. Everyone else seems to have forgotten it."

Jeremiah closed his eyes and remained silent. He opened his eyes.

"I am ready to die for the truth if I have to," he said.

Nostrum stopped bouncing one thumb off the other.

"Jeremiah, I don't know if this is going to work. But we can give it a try." He pushed his chair over to where Jeremiah was seated.

"Do you see that picture on the wall behind me?"

"Yes," said Jeremiah.

"Good. Do you see the handle of the cup?"

"Yes," said Jeremiah.

"Good. I want you to concentrate on that handle and not take your eyes off it."

Jeremiah did as he was told.

"You can hear me but you can't see me," said Nostrum. "I am looking at your left hand. I am staring at it. I can see it rising on its own with no help from you. You cannot stop it. Your hand is starting to move on its own. Little by little it is rising. That is good. Your hand is getting higher and higher. Very good. Now your hand is starting to get heavy, very heavy, too heavy to hold up. It is starting to move downward, very slowly, very slowly. When it touches the arm of your chair you will be asleep. Good, Jeremiah. Very good. Can you hear me?"

"Yes," said Jeremiah.

"Good. Jeremiah, did you have an attic in the house where you grew up?"

"Yes."

"Good. I want you to go up into that attic, Jeremiah, and tell me what you see."

Jeremiah told him everything he saw.

"Jeremiah. That attic is your mind, filled up with clutter and debris from your past. We need to clean it out completely. Work your way from one corner to the other. Describe to me everything you do."

Jeremiah did as instructed. He swept out every corner. He swept along the baseboard. He swept between every crack in the floor. Then he threw out the old, moth-eaten furniture. He threw out the curtains. He ripped up the old, urine-stained carpet and threw that out. He threw out the piles of old newspapers stacked in one corner. He threw out the old letters he had been saving, throwing and sweeping until there was nothing left in his mind of everything that had mattered to him and that he had all along called his life.

"Good. Very good," said Nostrum. "Your mind is completely empty. There is nothing there to control or influence you in any way. You in your conscious mind will decide what you want to do and you will do it. You are free. Do you hear me?"

"Yes," said Jeremiah.

"Good," said Nostrum. "Now count from one to ten with me. At ten you will be awake and you will forget everything that just happened."

Jeremiah counted to ten and opened his eyes. He exhaled slowly. That was his old life in winding sheets leaving his body forever.

It was on a crisp autumn day in early October, about two weeks before the critical debate between himself and the president, that Jeremiah finally started to catch on to truth telling. He was standing on the top step of Bryant Park at 42nd Street and Sixth Avenue, addressing a throng of lunchtime strollers who were slowing down just a little bit to hear what the candidate had to say for himself. He began simply.

"I'm a liar, and I have been all my life," he said. That stopped a lot of people dead in their tracks. They wanted to hear more.

"It's all I've known. It's all I've understood. I want to try and do something different – speak the truth – but I'm not sure I know how to do it. What about you, sir," he asked a well-dressed man in his sixties, "are you a liar like me?"

"Well...I...Uh," the man fumbled for words, taken aback by Jeremiah's directness, uncomfortable with the eyes upon him. "I suppose so. I always tell people I love what I do for a living. That's a lie. I say I'm happy. That's not true. I listen to candidates like you and make believe that the system is working. That's a lie – " He was ready to go on and on.

"Thank you," said Jeremiah, cutting him off and turning to address an attractive, flashily dressed woman in her twenties.

"What about you, miss?"

"I'm a whore," she answered in a straightforward way. "I screw for a living and have to make believe I care about the Johns who dick me, or they won't pay. But at least I know I'm lying. I'll bet the rest of you can't say that."

"And you, sir," said Jeremiah, pointing to a middle-aged construction worker.

"I've been cheating on my wife with the same woman for the past twelve years. The lie is that I love either one of them."

"So we're all liars, aren't we?" said Jeremiah. "But where does lying get us? We're miserable wretches anyway. Maybe it's time to give truth a chance."

Jeremiah paused, sensing he had the crowd with him.

Then, as if it were planned, though it wasn't, a bearded college student, waved his fist into the air and yelled out, "No More Lies! No More Lies!"

At first there was quiet. Then some other voices joined in. "No More Lies." Soon the entire crowd was chanting as Jeremiah hammered out the cadence.

"NO MORE LIES. NO MORE LIES. NO MORE LIES."

By this time a large number of people had gathered. The crowd was overflowing into the street and blocking traffic. A police car stopped. One of the officers got out.

"Come on, let's go. Break it up," he said, nudging people back onto the sidewalk with his night stick. Reluctantly the crowd began to disperse. Those who could get near him thanked Jeremiah, shaking his hand and assuring him he had their votes. Jeremiah felt light as air.

News spread fast about what had happened that day on the corner of 42nd Street and Sixth Avenue. The phrase "No More Lies" was catching on like brushfire in autumn. Board meetings on Wall Street, school board meetings, Sunday morning sermons, presidential, congressional, senatorial, mayoral, and pastoral news conferences were all being interrupted with the same unrelenting chant – "NO MORE LIES." Jeremiah had started something that quickly was beyond his control. CRAP was worried. Treason told Nick to cancel all appearances.

"What's going on?" said Jeremiah to Nick. "This is not the time to pull back. I can't do anything wrong. In fact, I'm finally doing everything right. The unthinkable might happen. I might actually be elected on the 'Truth Ticket.' Don't you realize what that would do for this country and the world? How can you let yourself get in the way?"

"It's not me," said Nick. "I don't have the money. I don't make the rules. CRAP does."

"We are there already. We don't need their money. I could raise whatever money I wanted in my own name."

"That wouldn't be wise. This is business, Jeremiah. We agreed to work for CRAP. I don't think they would tolerate our going our own way."

"Too bad for them," said Jeremiah.

Despite his lying, Jeremiah had never really lost his innocence. He had never bought into the system. He was playing at a game that he had invented and playing it out in his own private world. Thus, he was in much greater danger than he realized.

"They will kill you for sure," said Meghan, passing through the living room on the way to the kitchen.

"Maybe they will," he said.

CHAPTER 3 2

October 20, 2004

THE DAY OF THE long-awaited debate arrived. Jeremiah's ratings were on the rise. He and the president were about even. The debate would decide it all.

Jeremiah had been instructed to start lying again. The truth had gotten out of hand. Meghan convinced him to comply. To his misfortune, the president, who did not learn about this reversal in his opponent's strategy until it was too late, believed it was time for him to stop lying and start telling the truth.

Warned against looking too good and upstaging the president, Jeremiah came unshaven, with tousled hair, dressed in a day-old shirt and pants with no crease. As it turned out women found this bedroom look appealing.

The president won the toss and was the first to go.

"It's not easy being rich," began the president, nervously adjusting his note cards, clearly not at home with the truth. "It's not easy. I know a lot of rich people and I'm pretty darned rich myself. And let me tell you, being rich isn't all it's cracked up to be."

He seemed to relax a little.

"A lot of my rich friends are having quite a tough time of it. And what bothers the heck out of me," he said, with a look of disdain in Jeremiah's direction, as if he were responsible, "is that everybody thinks it's a joke. Well, let me tell you, it's not a joke. It's not funny at all."

The president was starting to get the hang of it.

"Does anyone really care about the rich? Does anyone worry about what happens to them? No, and that's a darn shame. Because rich people have feelings, too. I think we sometimes forget that. And the rich also have rights. Sure, they are a minority. But are we the kind of people to turn our backs on minorities? Or are we the kind of people to reach out with a helping hand?"

Here he made a gesture with his right hand.

"There is a lot of talk about 'poverty,' and 'the poor.' Well I'm all for poverty, and I think my record shows it. But when was the last time you heard someone speak out on the 'plight of the rich'?"

The president then went on to explain everything he had done for the rich in his first four years and everything he was going to be doing for them in the next four.

"Over the past four years you've all been making sacrifices for the rich. And I just want to say 'Thank you' from all of us. But there are some hard times ahead. And I know you are not the kind of people to walk out on your friends, to back down on a commitment, or to quit when the going gets tough. So, we're counting on you to live through a little bit more unpleasantness in the next four years so we rich can enjoy the comforts we've grown accustomed to."

Here, the president paused for applause and was greeted with a stony silence. Undaunted, he continued down the same track.

"Now there are those who say, 'The rich are bleeding the economy.' Well that's true. We all know that.

"There are those who say, 'We are destroying the earth to save the rich.' Well that's true, too. We all know that.

"There are those who say, 'It's not fair. We pay all the taxes and the rich get all the benefits.' Well, that's true. We all know that."

The president then went on to list numerous such "truths," a litany of sacrifices, a catechism of suffering which the nonrich were to endure on behalf of the rich, ending each item, in a liturgical whine, with the phrase, "We all know that."

Apparently, however, this was not the kind of truth the American people were interested in hearing. They were turning their television sets off by the millions. The president's campaign manager was waving frantically to try and get him to change his course, but the president stubbornly insisted on telling the truth. By the time it was Jeremiah's turn to make his opening remarks, the debate was already over. He had won, hands down. There was nothing he could do or say that would change that.

The following day the polls showed Jeremiah to have 55 percent of the vote and the president, still slipping, with only 45 percent. This was serious. Many of the politicos on both sides who had thought that Jeremiah was just a stalking-horse were now beginning to accept the reality that he would, indeed, be the next president of the United States, and they wanted to be sure they were on the bandwagon.

Jeremiah's phone was ringing off the hook with calls from people who claimed to be old friends and longtime supporters who wanted to know if there was anything they could do to help out. One of them was from Cawley Watson, who, apologizing for underestimating Jeremiah's potential, explained that he was throwing the full weight of his organization behind Jeremiah and that he was counting on Jeremiah's winning. Jeremiah thanked him for his support.

The contest was turning out to be so lopsided that news media analysts were worried that no one would even bother turning on his set to watch election-eve forecasts. CRAP was in a stew, and what's more, there was no one to blame. Jeremiah was doing exactly as told. That, it turned out, was the problem. Getting desperate and just a little reckless, they came up with yet another ploy. Jeremiah was to issue a position paper, a white paper, which was so ludicrous and offensive that it would convince voters that Jeremiah was off his rocker and unfit for higher office. CRAP didn't care what it was, just so long as it was preposterous enough.

Jeremiah, Nick and Meghan met at Nika's for a brainstorming session.

"Anything goes. Absolutely anything. The wackier, the better," said Jeremiah.

"All right," Nick said, "if that's the case, why don't we just do away with elections altogether. How about that?"

"Great," said Jeremiah, jotting it down on his yellow lined pad. "No elections. All right, then what?"

"Then ... then we draw straws," said Meghan.

"Right. I like that," said Jeremiah.

"A lottery," Nick said. "Anyone, absolutely anyone, can serve in government, from the lowliest of college professors all the way up to the guy who slices boiled ham at the corner deli."

"Well," said Meghan, "suppose we do away with both houses and the presidency and replace it all with government by council. That way we get everyone in on the act. Let's say there's a department of education," she said. "Suppose we duplicate that department in every congressional district in the country. That makes 435 councils of education at the local level. Let's say twelve members in each council chosen by lot —"

"We'll put an expert on each particular subject — education, health, foreign affairs, etc. — in each of the respective councils and someone who knows how to lead discussions," said Jeremiah. "These will be open debates. Anyone can come and address the council or just sit and listen."

"Then," Nick said, "let's say each council chooses from its members a representative who goes to Washington with the education proposal it has hammered out. And then there is a meeting of these 435 selected education council members who then agree on a joint proposal that is put before the entire electorate. A referendum."

"Yes," said Meghan, "a computer and a modem in every home, all tied into this vast computer network with a signed voting card – like a credit card. You just slip your plastic voting card past a magnetic scanner that reads your number and signature, and records your vote. Everyone votes on these proposals without even leaving their home."

"And there are different councils for every department of government: banking, defense, highways, health, environment, foreign affairs, etc.," said Jeremiah.

"And there's a Council of Councils," said Meghan, "made up of one representative from each of the departments, selected from among the Washington councils for that department. Let's say there are about twelve departments, which means about twelve members in this Council of Councils who choose one of their members to be their spokesperson. She –"

"Or he," said Nick, raising an eyebrow.

"He or she," Meghan corrected herself, "is the symbolic spokesperson and leader of the country. Everyone serves one two-year term on a staggered basis. That way there's some overlap."

"I think we've got it," said Jeremiah. "All we need is a name. We have to call it something. Something catchy."

"Why not just call it 'Democracy,' " said Meghan, resting her cup of coffee in its saucer and wiping her lips with a napkin. "That's simple. Democracy."

"I like it," said Jeremiah. "I like it. But they'll never buy it."

Jeremiah was dead wrong. The man in the street, scholarly journals, the public at large, media, the talk shows – everyone was discussing Jeremiah's new proposal. It was the first original political idea in two hundred years and had captivated the public's imagination.

No one had ever really thought about democracy before and everyone was fascinated and titillated by what it might mean. People started inventing their own versions, and in no time flat, there was a boardgame called "Democracy," a nail polish called "Democracy," a TV game show called "Democracy," and a moving company called "Democracy Movers – We Move Everyone Everywhere."

Jeremiah was in big trouble.

CHAPTER 33

October 21, 2004

CRAP DECIDED THAT IT was time for Frank Treason and wavy-haired Bob himself to meet with the campaign staff at the 57th Street headquarters. Jeremiah had never met Bob before and really had very little understanding about what CRAP was and what it was up to.

The atmosphere was tense and somber. Bob did his best to lighten things up. Treason was as quiet and humble as a schoolboy in the principal's office.

"Well, I want to tell you, Jeremiah," Bob began, once everyone was seated, "that you have a great deal of ability and that what you have accomplished is most impressive."

He furrowed his brow and tilted his head in a gesture of sincerity.

"But, Jeremiah, that's me. I'm just speaking for myself, when I say this. I have to think of the others at CRAP, as well, and they don't think – now I'm speaking for them, Jeremiah, I hope you understand that – you can restore the presidency to what it was under Hoover and Coolidge which, after all, is what CRAP is all about. The stakes are high and there is too much to lose."

"So you want me to take a fall," said Jeremiah, for the first time seeing clearly how he had been used and realizing that he had no choice in the matter.

"I'm not sure that is exactly the way I'd put it," said Bob. "It really isn't about taking a fall. It is about what is best for the country."

"All right," said Jeremiah. "I can do that."

"Well," said Bob, clearly relieved, "so you understand that we really have to do something to make sure you lose. We have to do something that completely alienates the electorate, that makes them angry with you, outraged that they had ever thought of voting for you. We need some good ideas," he said, surveying the group.

There was silence, made uneasy by Bob's menacing affability.

"Suppose I make a major address, over nationwide television," said Jeremiah, looking at his right hand which he was closing and opening in a rhythmical fashion, "and begin by blowing my nose into the American flag. That ought to do it."

The group seemed to relax, as if one.

"You're right," said wavy-haired Bob, looking very pleased. "I think it will."

The details were ironed out. Bob brought the discussion to a close. He was determined to get the others to warm up to him and so invited himself and Frank to dinner. Sarah prepared an excellent meal of scallops and leeks in a champagne and black mushroom sauce over a bed of cellophane noodles. Wavy-haired Bob and Frank ate with gusto and did their best to keep the conversation going. Jeremiah and company had long faces and little appetite.

Finally Bob and Frank left. Meghan excused herself and went back to Yonkers, leaving Jeremiah and Nick to themselves. The two hadn't been alone together since the campaign madness had begun.

"You knew all along that this was a setup," Jeremiah said, not bothering to look at Nick.

"Yes, I did," Nick said, not caring to defend himself.

"Nick," said Jeremiah, looking him square in the eye, "you are a prick. You really are a prick."

For the first time since he had known Jeremiah, Nick actually respected him.

CHAPTER 34

Sunday Morning, October 24, 2004

THE DAY OF THE major address arrived. It was on Sunday morning, nine days before the election. Just to be safe, Jeremiah decided to speak on the subject of religion to a live audience of bishops, priests, ministers and rabbis in a way that would be just as offensive, if not more so, than his blowing his nose in the American flag.

For the occasion, an eight-foot by ten-foot flag was suspended low and just behind the lectern, ostensibly serving as a backdrop for Jeremiah.

Before beginning, as if to build to the moment, he turned to look at the flag and seemed to be making a face, as if in disgust. This was clearer to the televison audience, than to the live audience, who did not notice anything unusual.

Then, casually, Jeremiah walked over to the flag, picked up one of the corners and wiped the perspiration off his forehead.

"Hey, don't do that," said the cameraman, followed by a chorus of "Don't do that," "What's the matter with you?" and "Show some respect."

Jeremiah returned to the lectern as if to begin. The hubbub subsided. Jeremiah started sniffling. He stopped to search his pocket for a handkerchief and found none. Then he turned to the flag, paused for a moment, looked at the flag and, his back to his audience, reached over, took one of the edges in his hand and with a loud snort, blew his nose into the American flag.

Mayhem followed. Everyone was out of his seat, charging toward the stage and screaming Jeremiah's name. "Stop him." "Get him." "Kill him." "Crucify him." "Flay him alive." "Boil him in oil." One rabbi took his belt off and fashioned it into a noose.

Wavy-haired Bob, who was present for the event, climbed onto the stage and spoke to the mob of peace-loving religious zealots.

"Please, everyone, please. Let's settle down. Let's hear what the candidate has to say."

The group responded to Bob's soothing manner, returned to their seats and gradually calmed down.

"There is no God," began Jeremiah, once there was complete quiet, "we all know that," deliberately using the president's phrase and imitating his liturgical whine. The crowd once again rose to its feet and began screaming.

Jeremiah paused and, finding no opening, continued anyway.

"Man invented God, not the other way round," he said, straining to speak over the noise.

He had to speak louder and louder to be heard.

"Then greedy sycophants and demagogues like yourselves came along."

He could barely hear his own words.

"You saw religion for the piece of pie it was. You took it and made it your own, in one of the biggest grabs for power and wealth in the history of civilization," he screamed over the shouting.

The din was painfully loud and overpowering. The crowd was menacing and dangerous. A cordon of guards had to keep the audience at bay. Wavy-haired Bob escorted Jeremiah off the stage to a torrent of epithets, screams, boos, catcalls, whistles and foot-stomping.

The event was a total failure, which is to say, a brilliant success.

The voters were angry, all right, damned angry. They had had it. But they were also dizzy and confused. They didn't know what to think or whom to believe. Pollsters were not even getting a foot in the door. Americans wanted no part of politics. CRAP had lost control of events. It was an open election. Anything could happen.

CHAPTER 35

The Week Before the Election

JEREMIAH WAS DISGUSTED WITH himself. Having just begun his jour-ney down the path to righteousness, he had briefly experienced that feeling of exaltation which comes from speaking the truth. Then he had thrown it all away in a cheap performance designed to manipulate an unsuspecting electorate. Nothing that anyone said seemed to make him feel any better.

Sarah cooked him miso soup and shrimp in black bean sauce, one of his favorites. He poked at his food and left most of it. Nick took him for a ride in the Ferrari down to the Jersey Shore, hoping that a view of the ocean and a walk along the beach would bring him back to life. They were silent most of the way, even though for some strange reason it seemed as if Jeremiah actually forgave Nick for betraying him.

"I'm really no better," said Jeremiah. "In fact, I'm much worse. You betrayed and exploited me. I betrayed and exploited an entire nation."

Jeremiah spent most of the week following his nose-blowing performance out at Meghan's place in Yonkers, gathering and peeling apples, raking leaves, and playing with dolls, blocks and cars with Kelly. After almost four days in this therapeutic milieu, he was starting to come around.

But all good things must come to an end. CRAP decided it was time for Jeremiah to address a restless public, which certainly hadn't lost interest in him as a national figure. In fact, he was more talked about now than ever. Once again, however, he would have to compromise himself so as to placate CRAP and extricate himself from a delicate situation.

After a three-hour meeting with Frank and Bob it was decided that Jeremiah would hold a news conference. The possibility of his resigning his candidacy and throwing his full support behind the president was discussed. But that would have created enormous complications. First of all, the ballots had been made up. There was no way new ballots could be created and distributed before the election. Secondly, there had never in the history of the republic been an election with only one presidential candidate. Such an occurrence would reveal the process to be the fraud it was, bringing into question the legitimacy of the presidency itself which, needless to say, was the exact opposite of what CRAP had in mind. No, that definitely would not do. Jeremiah would have to remain a candidate. Without actually saying so, he was to imply his wish that voters choose the incumbent. This was a last-ditch effort. No one was optimistic about its potential effectiveness.

"No one is going to buy it," said Nick as he, Jeremiah and Meghan took a leisurely walk through Central Park.

"Maybe I should just tell them the whole story. That would certainly grab some headlines," said Jeremiah.

Meghan took Jeremiah by the arm.

"It's almost over," she said, trying to steer him in a different direction. "Soon you'll have your life back. Think of what you'll be doing next."

Jeremiah's mood seemed to brighten. Maybe it was time to write a book. Maybe even a novel. He became more animated as he spoke and started working out the story line with the help of his two friends. He resolved himself to playing out the last act at the news conference and then starting something new.

The apartment at 57th Street was filled with reporters talking amongst themselves in a whisper. Jeremiah appeared and was introduced by wavy-haired Bob. There was tension in the room.

"In the course of this rigorous campaign," Jeremiah began, on the Friday before the election, "I have learned a lot, not only about myself and the American electorate, but about the president himself. While I had always considered him a worthy adversary, my respect for him has actually increased in these difficult months."

Jeremiah looked towards Bob, who gave him a nod of approval.

"Here is a man who can speak the truth," he continued. "Here is a man who has strong allegiances and a sense of commitment. Here is a man who takes care of himself and his rich friends who have as much right to representation as the poor, the middle class, or the migrant workers who can't even vote anyway."

Bob, who tried to lead a round of applause, was a lone clapper.

"And how many of us really appreciate how much we owe the rich? It is thanks to their profligate spending that many of us have jobs. It is thanks to their philanthropy that we have museums and libraries and magnificent decaying mansions along the Hudson River that we can visit on a Sunday afternoon. They give us glamour and glitter, a way of life we can admire from afar. For this we owe them much. And any man who, as president, is willing to unabashedly devote his efforts to their welfare is a worthy man, indeed."

Jeremiah was interrupted by a flurry of questions.

"Are you saying that voters should choose your opponent?" asked one attractively dressed woman reporter.

"I'm not saying that," said Jeremiah. "I'm simply saying that he has earned my respect over the course of this campaign."

"Isn't it unusual at this stage of a campaign to start praising one's adversary?" asked another veteran Washington reporter with a Southern accent.

"Perhaps it is. But perhaps campaigns in the past have been too bitter and divisive," replied Jeremiah.

"There is talk that this whole thing is a hoax," said another reporter, a young man with shaggy red hair, "that you were just put up as a stalking-horse to ensure the incumbent's victory, that you ended up doing better than you were supposed to and that now you're trying to throw the election. Is there any truth to any of that?"

"That is totally preposterous," said Jeremiah, taken aback by the reporter's audacity. "I think you have disgraced yourself and the president by even making such a suggestion."

The room was quiet. Jeremiah was on the spot. Wavy-haired Bob stepped in, explained that Jeremiah had a busy schedule, that that was all he had time for and wouldn't everyone stay for some vodka and caviar. The conference ended on a note of ambiguity and distrust.

Bob and Frank ushered Jeremiah and Nick into one of the bedrooms.

"Good job," said Bob with his mouth. With his eyes, he said, "You're in trouble." Frank said nothing and looked frightened.

"No more public appearances," said Bob. "Stay out of sight." He rested his hand momentarily on the sleeve of Jeremiah's jacket and then turned to leave.

"You'll be hearing from us," he said mechanically, and then he was gone.

CHAPTER 36

That Evening

EVERYONE HAD AN OMINOUS feeling. No one said anything. Jeremiah went back to his place. Meghan left for Yonkers. Nick found himself a bar on Eighth Avenue. He was feeling grim. A woman in her forties with tan, leathery skin, bleached-blond hair, and gold jewelry from head to foot turned her head to size him up.

"Hi, beautiful," she said in a hoarse voice as she cradled her drink in both hands.

Nick sat down at the bar.

"What'll it be?"

The bartender was over six feet, had square features. His hair was pulled back in a pony tail. He wore a waste-high, clean white apron. He leaned against the edge of the bar with two hands. Taking Nick's lack of response for indecision, he turned around and walked to the other end of the bar.

"This," he said, pointing to a bottle of Glenlivet, "is Christ reborn. It has a deep, spiritual meaning. It will take you out of your body, ever so gently and then bring you back again into a body that has been reconstituted. It will glue back together what has become unglued. This," he said, pointing to a bottle of Glenfiddich two rows up, "is a completely different story. This is lithe and supple. A woman in a tight fitting gown. No joints. All movement. Non stop undulation..."

He paused for Nick's response.

"I'll take 'Christ reborn,'" he said.

The bartender carefully removed the bottle from the shelf, set down a glass and slowly, gently, so as not to damage the texture or fiber, poured a healthy offering. Like a midwife who has just delivered a baby and lovingly sets the newborn on its mother's belly, he took a step backwards and with his hands on his hips, waited for Nick's response.

Nick let out a sigh and picked up the glass. He took a small sip and let it settle in his mouth. At first he felt a sharp, unpleasant sensation. Then came a feeling of localized warmth which he didn't want to let go of.

"Swallow," the bartender said.

Nick swallowed, slowly and deliberately. It was as if warm velvet were being unrolled and spread across his body. Then came a sense of well-being which stretched on and on.

Nick raised his eyebrows and gave a slight smile.

Joe nodded his understanding.

Nick drank one and then another.

"Here," said Joe, placing a bottle of Glenlivet on the bar. "I'm not supposed to do this. But I'll sell you this one."

"Thanks," said Nick.

Something bad was about to happen. Nick was sure of it. But instead of doing something to try to stop it he was sitting in a bar by himself drinking Scotch and listening to vintage Sinatra over a loud jukebox.

He should have been with Jeremiah, but couldn't face him. Or was it that he couldn't face himself? Or was it that he sensed that there was nothing he could do, that he was up against something too mysterious and too powerful to comprehend or overcome?

There was a woman in her thirties sitting next to him at the bar. Somewhere out of middle America. Came to New York to make her career in the theater and hadn't yet made it but maybe had had a taste of it. Her face was heavy with make-up, getting ready for a rehearsal or just coming from one. There was a deep inner glow of sensitivity. She seemed sad.

"It couldn't be that bad," Nick said, looking her way.

She looked back with a smile and her plain features became ignited with passion and beauty.

"Do I seem sad?" she asked, looking at Nick with penetrating, dark brown eyes.

Nick felt himself losing power, becoming her helpless servant. *The Blue Angel,* he the fumbling, oafish professor doing her every bidding, she Marlene Dietrich, smoking cigars, flirting with bell-hops and businessmen, watching with amusement as he crawls across the floor at her heels.

"A little," Nick said, unable to take his eyes off hers. "Maybe you were just going over your lines."

"Richard told me I could come out to his place for the weekend if I wanted, but that Barbara also was going to be there."

"Who's Richard?"

"My lover."

"Who's Barbara?"

"The woman he's replacing me with," she said, her eyes glistening with raw emotion.

Nick wanted desperately to take her in his arms and comfort her.

"You shouldn't go," Nick said, almost trembling with concern. "You shouldn't go."

"I have to go," she said.

"Why?" Nick asked.

"Because I said I would." She pushed a ten-dollar bill across the bar and was getting ready to leave.

"Don't leave," Nick said.

"I have to get back to rehearsal. Don't worry, I'll do fine," she said, forcing a smile. "I always do."

Nick watched her walk towards the door, hoping she would turn around. She didn't.

He ordered another Scotch, handed the bartender a dollar and asked for some change for the phone.

"Janet, this is Nick," he said.

"Nick?" she asked. "Nick who?"

"Nick you-know-damned-well-who," he said.

"So let me guess. You're sitting at a bar. You're feeling lonely. You just had your second Scotch. Maybe you caught sight of some attractive woman who has stirred your passions and you're looking for a woman to hold. Do I have it right?"

"Pretty close," he said.

"Meet me over at Angela's in about twenty minutes," she said.

Angela's is a typical Yorkville invention, offering mediocre "American cuisine" in a modest setting for modest prices. It has been at the same location on York Avenue for the past twenty years, serving the same steaks, chops, roast beef and fried chicken, with a few pastas and salads having been added to the menu in homage to the current decade. The same ageless, heavyset waiters and waitresses have been there for as long as anyone can remember. This was Janet's home away from home. She ate there five nights a week and ordered Chinese or Italian take-out the other two. Janet had taken a vow against cooking.

Nick stopped at a local Korean market and picked up a bouquet of flowers for ten dollars and hid them on the seat next to him, holding them in reserve for the right moment.

He was early. Janet was late as always.

She looked pretty that night. She was wearing a white turtleneck, a gold chain, opal earrings. She sparkled.

"You look two-derful, three-night," Nick said in inflationary language.

Janet smiled and sat down.

Nick scanned the mind-numbing menu and then looked up at Janet in helpless bewilderment.

"Have the fried chicken," she said. "You always like that."

Janet ordered the chef's salad.

They groped for words. Janet worked as a buyer for Macy's and liked to talk shop. Her job took her overseas. She always had some interesting stories to tell. Nick kept encouraging her to talk more. He found it more interesting than he usually did. Anything he could think of talking about he wanted to forget.

"I have traveled to Indonesia," she said. "You wouldn't believe the conditions these people work in for thirty cents a day. Child labor. Enslavement."

"That's terrible," Nick said.

"We should be paying them a living wage. I am part of the system that makes the exploitation possible."

"Don't be hard on yourself," he said. "We all are."

Then she stopped short and started toying with her food.

"Nick, this isn't working."

"What isn't working?" Nick asked, knowing exactly what she had in mind.

"Us. It's not working."

"It's working just fine."

"Maybe it's working for you. It's not working for me. We're heading nowhere."

"Where's there to head? What's wrong with right here?"

"Nick, you've got a drinking problem."

"Drinking problem? I have no problem drinking. You should know that better than anyone," Nick bounced back. "And anyway, what's drinking got to do with it? The sex is great. Admit it."

"Nick, there is more to life than sex."

"Do you know that for sure?" asked Nick.

Clearly, she didn't.

"Nick," she said, "maybe we ought to call it a night." He had cut her off at every turn. That was probably a mistake.

"Here, these are for you," he said, taking the flowers out of their hiding place and holding them across the table.

Janet looked at the flowers admiringly. She sniffed them.

"The lilies smell so beautiful," she said.

She took his hand and gave it a squeeze.

"You look upset," she said. "It's the campaign, isn't it?"

"Why should I be upset?" he said, finishing off a glass of Scotch.

They took a dreamy walk back to Janet's place. At two in the morning Nick awoke and could not fall back to sleep. He got out of a warm, comfortable bed, and started getting dressed.

"Is something the matter?" Janet asked groggily.

"Nothing," said Nick. "I'll call you tomorrow."

CHAPTER 37

The Next Morning

A ROUND NINE O'CLOCK THE next morning the telephone rang.
His eyes still closed, Nick reached across the night table. Half a
glass of Glenlivet fell to the floor.

"Who the hell is this?" he grumbled.

"He's dead," said Meghan in a pinched voice. "Jeremiah … He's
dead," she said breaking down into sobs. "A pretzel vendor found
him around eight this morning. He was hanging from an elm tree
near Poet's Walk."

Nick said nothing. What came to mind was the Billie Holiday
song "Strange Fruit" and the image of a Southern lynching with the
Ku Klux Klan gathered round in white hooded sheets, the young
black hanging limply by the neck, barefoot, in a white T-shirt and
dungarees.

The silence lengthened. Meghan hung up with a loud click.

Nick let the receiver fall to his lap. He slipped down under the covers, and fell asleep to the sound of Maximum, his cat, licking up the Scotch.

Nick awoke some time later – it could have been a few minutes or an hour – to the whooping sound of a car alarm somewhere down the block.

Following him towards the kitchen was Maximum, ranging this way and that on limbs that seemed to be giving way from under him. A comic, yet pathetic sight. The Glenlivet. Nick filled the cat's dish with water and had to hold him upright so he could drink from it.

Nick opened the refrigerator and studied its contents. The orange juice caught his eye. Some secret meaning was contained therein. Strange fruit, he thought. Then it all came back to him, Jeremiah's hanging from the elm tree, Billie Holiday, that poor black boy, the Ku Klux Klan. What a terrible dream. Or was it? Maybe Meghan really did call.

Nick decided to play it safe.

It was about 10:45 A.M. by the time he got to Central Park. There were some stragglers pointing at a Dutch elm and quietly talking to each other. There were a couple of police cars parked at odd angles along the wide walk beside a statue of Walter Scott. A few officers were chatting idly. The top brass had come and gone. Seated on a bench, her arms folded, her shoulders scrunched forward against the cold was Meghan. Her eyes and nose were red. Her skin looked whiter than ever. She acknowledged Nick's presence without uttering a word.

Nick ignored the band of yellow tape – "Police Line Do Not Cross" – and kicked his way through a mixture of fallen leaves and candy wrappers looking for he didn't know what. It was a cold autumn morning. There was a slight breeze. He felt the chill.

It was only now, looking at the proud, lonely elm, cordoned off from the other elms by bands of yellow tape that it occurred to him that Jeremiah might actually be dead.

Nick ducked back under the tape and took in the scene. Not

179

many people. Not much activity. Nothing out of the ordinary. Then he realized he was looking at the pretzel vendor directly in front of him, about six feet across the walk.

"What happened?" Nick asked, pointing in the direction of the yellow tape.

The pretzel vendor tilted his head backward and pushed out his lips. Was he trying to figure out what Nick had said or was he trying to come up with an answer?

"The yellow tape. The cops. What happened?"

The vendor paused for a moment.

"He dead," he said, sucking in some air from the side of his mouth and then shrugging his shoulders. He seemed upset. "He hang. Zee tree." He tilted his head limply to one side. "He hang like dees."

There was no way Nick could ask him what the man looked like or how he was dressed. But he had to find out what he knew. He was sure the cops hadn't bothered to question him. Nick found himself speaking very slowly.

"Was...there...anything? Did...you...see...anything? Anything?"

The pretzel vendor thought for a moment, started shaking his head no and then caught himself. He touched his hand to the breast pocket of his jacket. "Papeer," he said.

"Paper," Nick repeated. "Thanks."

Nick walked over to the elm tree and began kicking up the leaves again, this time with a purpose. After about ten minutes he found a piece of paper with three words penciled in caps, "NO MORE LIES!"

Nick had a sinking feeling in the pit of his stomach.

"Shit," he said quietly, fighting back a couple of tears. "He's dead."

For a moment he didn't know what to do. Then he realized he had to get back to Jeremiah's place before the police did.

"Come on," he said to Meghan. He took her by the hand and led the way to Fifth Avenue, where he hailed a cab.

Meghan sat frozen on one side of the cab, Nick on the other. Nick felt he should say something.

"Meghan..." he began. The words wouldn't come.

They took the long ride without speaking.

It had been some time since Nick had seen the inside of Jeremiah's apartment.

"We shouldn't be here, Nick," said Meghan, as she followed him through the narrow entryway which also served as a kitchen.

The place seemed ever so quiet and homey. There was a soft breeze moving the gauze-like curtains. There was warm sunlight. There was quiet. There was almost a hint of domesticity about the place. Jeremiah was neat and organized. Books were well-ordered on the bookshelves by size and subject matter. There were a couple of interesting "artworks," i.e. some cheap reprints of Klee and several Degas drawings all attractively framed and thoughtfully placed on two walls. There was a large surface for writing, a handsome oak door atop two oak bookcases. The place almost had class.

"I didn't know Jeremiah liked art," said Meghan in front of one of the Degas.

"Jeremiah had an intellectual side. He kept it well-hidden," said Nick, looking out the window to a backyard of tall trees and planted gardens. A wave of melancholy washed over him. He took a seat in the one comfortable chair.

"Becoming president had been so important to him," said Nick. "And where did it get him? It got him a rope around his neck and a place in history. If that is what he wanted then he got what he came for."

Nick could feel himself fighting back the emotion.

Jeremiah kept notes, clippings and even audio cassettes on just about everything he ever read or thought. Nick wanted to find them and go through them before the police did. In an apartment the size of Jeremiah's there are very few hiding places. Nick found what he was looking for under the desk. There was a large carton filled with notepads, notebooks and sheets of paper of every size and description, each with something written on it in a legible hand, about a half dozen labeled manila files and about as many labeled audio cassettes. Without looking further Nick grabbed the carton, sagging and almost bursting from the weight of what it contained.

"Nick, you shouldn't be taking that," said Meghan.

"Why not? Who else would want it?"

"Maybe the police," said Meghan.

"It wouldn't mean anything to them," said Nick. "Come on."

They made it back to Nick's place and closed the door behind them. There were voices yelling back and forth and the clomping of feet up the stairs. The police. Nick held his breath as they passed the door, the carton still in his arms, as if he had committed a crime. But he hadn't. Or had he? Disturbing the scene of a crime. But it wasn't the "scene" of the crime. And who says disturbing the scene of a crime is a crime, assuming he had just disturbed it, which he hadn't really. And anyway who says there was a crime. Jeremiah supposedly hanged himself. Is that a crime?

Nick kicked away a pile of clothes and some old magazines from a corner near the window and quietly set the box down. There was a knock at the door. It was the police. Two expressionless cop faces, one full and puffy, the other nicely squared off and mean-looking.

How well did they know the deceased? One cop asking questions, the other taking notes, as if one cop couldn't undertake both assignments. Had they noticed anything strange about Mr. Greenfield? Would he have any reason to want to kill himself? Did he have any enemies? Was there anything unusual about his behavior? Nick offered as little as he could, though he really had nothing to withhold, other than the carton in the corner, which was none of their business, anyway. Meghan took the card that Officer Patrick Malloy handed her, thanked him and reassured him that should they have any additional information they would contact him.

"I think they know more than they're saying," said Nick. "Maybe they have doubts that it was a suicide."

"Who would go to Central Park to hang himself?" asked Meghan.

"Why not?" rejoined Nick. "It's a beautiful place to die."

CHAPTER 38

Around Noon

AFTER THE POLICE HAD left the building, Nick and Meghan were alone in the apartment with the carton of Jeremiah's writings. Nick poured himself a glass of Glenlivet, cleared a space next to the carton, sat down and started rummaging without any particular purpose in mind, handing to Meghan items he thought were of particular interest.

For a long time, he had been curious to learn about Jeremiah's network of secretaries. He had wanted to break the code. And there right in front of him was a carton of Jeremiah's writings filled with more secretarial secrets than he would know what to do with. But now it didn't seem to matter much one way or the other. Then again, maybe there would be some hint about who killed Jeremiah, assuming he hadn't killed himself.

Nick pushed the box towards the window where there was more

light. There were yellow lined pads, full-size spiral notebooks, small ones you could fit in your back pocket, notes written on loose scraps of paper, letters Jeremiah had received over the years bound together with rubber bands, audio cassettes, each carefully labeled. Crammed vertically along the side of Jeremiah's carton was an over-sized, impressive-looking envelope. Nick thought it was probably his high school diploma. Jeremiah saved everything. Nick opened the envelope and took out the document. It was Jeremiah's mar-riage certificate.

"I can't believe that he didn't shred it, ceremonially burnt it, or at least just throw it away," said Nick passing it along to Meghan.

In the same envelope with the marriage certificate was another, much smaller envelope, containing what looked like an invitation, which is what it was. Jeremiah had saved one of the invitations that Emma had sent out for her first and only "gala" dinner party for Maynard and Sissy.

"What an incredible sentimentalist," said Nick.

At the very bottom of the carton was a red leather, ledger-size binder. Nick worked it out from under the rest of the pile. It appeared to be a log of Jeremiah's Washington encounters, written in shorthand and code with the obvious intention of concealing from any chance reader like Nick the full meaning of what the entries meant. The first entry was dated June 9, 2003.

"'A.M. Crispy's 6:30 P.M. Blue Tie story. A.M. friends with A.B. Will set up a meeting. Expect a call.' To think that that story was the beginning of a notoriety which almost landed him in the White House," said Nick.

With the ledger opened in front of him Nick reached down into the carton and came up with a handful of paper, which he passed along to Meghan, scraps, notes written on napkins and on the backs of laundry tickets. None of it seemed to mean too much.

"What's this?" asked Meghan.

She held a piece of brown paper bag, with a column of initials on the left, arranged alphabetically by the first initial, and on the right a column of names, starting with "A.M.," Agnes McCauley and ending with "T.W.," Tina Walinsky. Holding the column of names alongside the ledger, Meghan deciphered the first entry.

"Meeting with Agnes McCauley at Crispy's. Agnes McCauley is a friend of Anna Bandolla."

"Anna Bandolla," said Nick. "That was the woman found floating down the Potomac."

Meghan picked her way through some more of the papers.

"I don't think Jeremiah ever really understood what he got himself into," she said.

"He didn't," said Nick.

"You did, though. Why didn't you help him?"

"Jeremiah got in over his head. It's a nasty world. There is nothing I can do about that," said Nick.

"You are part of that nasty world. Jeremiah wasn't. He trusted you."

"I made a deal," said Nick. "I had no way of knowing that this is how it would end up. He could have said no. We all have to live with our choices."

"Just what are *you* responsible for?" asked Meghan.

"Surviving, in a dog-eat-dog world," said Nick.

"Did you ever stop to think that maybe the world is the way it is because you are so busy surviving in it? Deep down inside you have a heart like the rest of us. No doubt it was broken a long time ago. I'll be in Yonkers if you need me," said Meghan, rising to leave. "Remember one thing. Jeremiah didn't drink to drown his sorrows. You do. Stay sober for a few days and let's see how tough you are."

"I'll think about that," said Nick, not bothering to get up.

CHAPTER 39

About 2:00 P.M. Nick's Apartment

THE PHONE RANG.

"This is Samantha Srongenson," said the airy wisp of a voice on the other end. "I'm looking for Jeremiah. I got your name from the *Ledger*."

Samantha Srongenson, probably part of Jeremiah's cabal, thought Nick. The president had ordered a news blackout so she would know nothing of Jeremiah's fate. Should he tell her that Jeremiah was no more or should he play her for what she was worth?

"Tell him I'll be standing outside Crispy's at six tonight," she said.

"Crispy's?" asked Nick.

"He'll know. It's not far from the National Gallery."

"I'll tell him," said Nick.

What the hell was he doing? Why hadn't he just told her? Now she would be waiting and he had no way of reaching her. Then again, here was a chance to satisfy his curiosity and meet one of these homely secretaries. It was the right thing to do. He'd tell her in person. Jeremiah had cashed in his chips.

On the plane ride to Washington, Nick thought about his conversation with Meghan. There was no way he could ever make her understand so he hadn't even bothered trying. She was hiding behind her high ideals just the way she accused him of hiding behind his booze. She would never grasp the subtle way events unfold, how one thing leads to another. Was he the first person to sell his soul for a few dollars? No. That is the way of the world. Wasn't he, Nicholas Belladonna, as much a victim of circumstances as Jeremiah? How could Meghan be so blind?

It was six-thirty by the time Nick found his way to Crispy's. There was no one waiting outside, so he decided to check inside. For the first time he realized that he didn't know what Samantha looked like. But he was sure he would recognize her when he saw her. He ordered a slice of pizza and a Coke. The place was filled with government workers, mostly women. It was easy to see how they could be organized into a ring of informants supplying Jeremiah with his inside Washington stories. Nick's appreciation for Jeremiah's ingenuity was rekindled. He scrutinized each newcomer with the hope that he would recognize Samantha. Maybe she was already there and he didn't know it.

Nick finished his pizza, paid his tab and walked out the side entrance that led to an alley. At first he saw nothing remarkable. There were garbage cans, cartons tied together for recycling, clear plastic bags filled with soda cans and glass bottles, some partially eaten slices of pizza. In a darkened corner, hidden by overgrowth, propped up against a red brick wall, in a lavender dress, wearing a pair of Reeboks, with buck teeth and a lousy case of acne, was Samantha – Nick was sure of it – her eyes bulging out, a pair of panty hose wrapped around her neck.

He looked to make sure no one was watching, walked up to the brick wall and put his hand against her cheek. Her skin was cold. He took a few steps backward.

Should he say something to someone inside? Should he call the police? If he did, would they ask questions that he would have a hard time answering? Samantha had probably found out about CRAP. Maybe she knew about Nick's involvement. Maybe she knew more than Nick knew. Was there any connection with Jeremiah's death and if there were, where would that put Nick? Nick reached into his pocket for some Glenlivet and took two long swallows. He walked casually back into the pizza place, ordered another slice and sat down at a table.

"You Greenfield's friend?" asked an Italian with flour on his hands.

Nick nodded.

"Heah, dis is fuh u," he said, dropping an envelope on the table.

The envelope had Jeremiah's name on the front. Nick opened it. Scribbled hastily on a crumpled piece of paper were the words, "WATCH OUT N.B.S.S." Nick repeated the letters to himself several times – "N.B.S.S." – and came up with nothing. He put the piece of paper in his pocket, ate the pizza and took a cab to the airport, doing his best to forget what he had just seen and what it might mean.

CHAPTER 40

The Following Day

ON MONDAY, NOVEMBER 1, 2004 televisions and radios across the nation were crackling with the news of Jeremiah's demise. Apparently, a graduate student from Columbia University had been in the park at about the time Jeremiah's body was discovered, though he wasn't really the one to discover it.

As he tells it, he was jogging past Poet's Walk around eight in the morning. He almost ran into a French family – mother, father and young boy – stopped in the middle of the road taking a picture. He turned to see what was so interesting and saw something hanging from a tree but couldn't make out exactly what it was. He jogged on. Then he had second thoughts and reversed his direction. From a distance he saw a pretzel vendor, looking both ways and then emptying the figure's pockets. It was at this point that the graduate student found the nearest phone and called the police.

The French family learned of the bizarre event the following day when the story was spread across the front page of every New York newspaper once the blackout had been lifted. They handed in the roll of film to the authorities who released the photo to the media. It provided an excellent front page shot of Jeremiah, under the banner headline, "PRESIDENTIAL CANDIDATE A SUICIDE."

The public was both titillated and terrified by Jeremiah's death. There was ghoulish fascination with the disturbing, though peaceful, image of Jeremiah hanging from an elm tree. There was endless discussion about what might have driven him to do it. There was speculation that it was not a suicide at all, but that Jeremiah had been assassinated and that the police had participated in a cover-up.

Brian Donne, the young reporter with shaggy red hair who had suggested at Jeremiah's last news conference that perhaps the whole election was a fraud, was interviewing anyone whom he could get a hold of. The French family, who had been interviewed briefly on television under strict supervision, was being held in isolation in the French embassy.

Was it a suicide? Was it a murder? If it was a suicide where was the note or the rational? All this doubt and uncertainty simply served to whet the public's appetite for more information. And there were broader questions – some of them quite far-ranging and disturbing in their implications – raised by television news commentators and newspaper editorialists. "What is happening to America?" "What is happening to her political system?" "What is the source of all this violence, self-inflicted or otherwise?" Previous assassinations were recalled with sadness and despair.

On Tuesday, November 2, the day of the election, Jeremiah was buried. This was a small, private, graveside affair. Over Meghan's protests Jeremiah's mother took complete charge. She insisted there be a rabbi. She invited distant and antiquated relatives, and had a modest buffet back at her place. The father, who had done everything he could to crush his only son, was the most voluble mourner.

As often happens at funerals, there was lightness mixed in with the grief. Mourners, relieved of their burden of sadness, were momentarily freed of their fear of death. Daily matters seemed less worrisome. At such times there is clarity of thought and openness to new ideas. People become philosophical. It is as if the passing of one soul makes extra room for those left behind.

Emma was off to one side, talking to Nick. Maynard had flown up from Alabama. Sissy had come in from New Jersey. She was engaged to be married.

"Good for you," said Maynard, giving her a hug, seeming to care for her now more than he ever had.

Maynard, himself, had found a mate, a black woman, who could not make it to the funeral.

"She's pregnant," he said with pride.

More congratulations and hugs.

Meghan introduced herself to Sissy.

"Jeremiah had so many good things to say about you," Meghan said in a plaintive way. Sissy gave her a hug.

Silence descended upon the group. Maynard began sobbing.

"He was a good person," he said. "Filled with enthusiasm. Never said anything bad about anyone. But, then…I don't know… Something happened. He started fading. But I can't believe he killed himself."

"Do you really think he did?" asked Sissy.

"I don't know what to think."

"He didn't kill himself," said Meghan, her lips set in bitter sorrow. "He loved me. He never would have left me. They wanted him out of the way."

"Who?" asked Maynard.

"The CRAP people,' said Meghan. "Ask Nick."

Nick turned his head but made no effort to join the group.

"It didn't have to be this way," said Sissy. "He was good, very good at what he did. If only he could have settled down."

"He wanted something bigger," said Maynard. "I did, too. I know what that is like."

"Life is not about something bigger," said Sissy. "It's about what happens every day."

"Some people get tired of what they have every day," said Nick, swiveling his chair in her direction.

"That's because they are dead inside," said Sissy.

Nick turned back the other way.

"Maybe so," said Meghan. "Or maybe they have a vision of a better world.'

"I wish that were true," said Sissy. "But so often the vision is of fame and glory. The world comes in a distant second."

"Jeremiah really started to see something," Meghan persisted. "I know he did. He got beyond himself. When he started speaking the truth, he changed. And he could see that he was changing others as well. That's why I know he didn't kill himself. He had found what he was looking for."

"Maybe he found the truth and couldn't live with it," said Maynard. "I don't think I could."

Nick and Emma got up to leave.

"Emma," said Sissy, "give me a call before you go back to Florida. We'll get together."

"I tried," said Emma, feeling a need to explain herself. "He wasn't easy to live with."

No one responded.

"Let's go," said Nick. "It's getting late."

CHAPTER 41

Several Weeks Later

ON A FRIDAY, TOWARD the end of November, a little more than three weeks after Jeremiah's death, Nick got a phone call. It was Officer Franco Follanico, the squared-off, mean-looking one who actually turned out to be a nice guy.

"Say, how's it goin' Mistuh Belladonna?" he said, straight out of Bensonhurst or Staten Island.

Nick was taken by surprise. He couldn't imagine what they wanted of him, and was feeling awkward trying to make small talk with a police officer.

"I'm fine, Officer Follanico, how are you?"

"Listen, we wuz sittin' around da office bullshittin' tryin' to figya out what da hell happened to dis poor Greenfield guy and your name pops up. 'Maybe Belladonna could help us out.'"

"So you want me to come down for a chat," Nick volunteered.

"Yea, a chat. Dats it, a chat."

They agreed on a time and said good-bye. Nick absent-mindedly hung up the phone, trying to figure out what the call was all about. The police were on to something. Did it involve Nick directly? He had nothing to hide. Then it came to him. That damned carton with Jeremiah's things in it. That was something to hide. Why was it in his apartment? Why did he sneak it out of Jeremiah's? Was he trying to conceal something? He had to get rid of that carton.

The simplest thing to do would be to return the carton to Jeremiah's apartment. That way there would be nothing to lie about and nothing to hide. Then, as he was bending down to pick it up, he realized that there actually might be something in the carton that could be incriminating. There was a lot to go through. He really didn't have the time or the patience to go through all of it. Nick randomly grabbed at a couple of things. Right on the top, under one of the spiral notebooks was an envelope. He opened it. The cryptic message Samantha had left at Crispy's the day he went to meet her. "WATCH OUT. N.B.S.S." He couldn't make it out then and couldn't make it out now.

He wrote the letters out in various combinations, starting from either end and then the middle. An obvious breakdown was, "N.B.," "S.S.," "S.S.," that's Samantha Srongenson. But "N.B.," what was that? "N.B." could mean *note bene* but made no sense in this context. And *note bene* probably was not in Samantha's lexicon. "N.B., N.B.," Nick repeated the letters out loud to himself several times. Then it came to him "N.B." was Nick himself, "Nicholas Belladonna."

"HOLY SHIT!" said Nick out loud.

Samantha was trying to warn Jeremiah. She had probably found out about Nick's connection to CRAP. Maybe she heard that they were out to get Jeremiah and thought that Nick was in on it. He had to get rid of the note.

Nick had never before been faced with getting rid of a piece of paper and leaving absolutely no trace. It is not such a simple matter. The most obvious thing to do is to crumple it up and throw it in the garbage. Except that is the first place the police would look.

In fact, maybe they called him just to get him in motion and reveal what he was hiding. He could shred it into small pieces and then throw it away. But they could find the pieces and then put them back together. He could burn the note. But just as he set it aflame there would be a knock at the door. There would be an odor. What was he doing? There would be ashes. He could throw them out the window. Some cop might be there watching.

Nick realized that the only intelligent thing to do was to take the note, put it back in the envelope and bury it in the box. The likelihood that the police would find it and make any sense out of it was not too great. At least, Nick could honestly claim, under oath, that he had destroyed no evidence.

Nick picked up the carton, opened the door, looked both ways and then hurried down the hall to the back stairs. No one saw him. He rested the box in front of Jeremiah's door and groped for the keyhole. The halls were poorly lit. His arm brushed against a heavy metal object. The door had been padlocked and an official notice from the sheriff's office glued to the door. In a panic, Nick picked up the carton and hurried back up the stairs. A cold sweat broke out on his neck and down his back. He made it to his floor and was about twenty feet from his apartment when a door opened.

"Hi," said a friendly voice straight out of Michigan, "I see you're moving, too." Flat chest, nice athletic body in her Spandex running shorts, baseball cap, with her pony tail bobbing up and down out the back. She must have moved in while Nick was living at 57th Street.

"Not really moving," said Nick, laughing loudly, "Ha, Ha," and talking too much. "Actually, I had been cleaning out my apartment and was taking this carton down to throw it out, but then I realized I really I hadn't gone through what was in it and decided to take it back upstairs just to make sure there wasn't anything I really wanted you know how sometimes the minute you throw something out that is the very thing you wish you had."

"I know just what you mean," she said, her "A's" as flat as her chest, one hand on her hip, the other cutting air for emphasis. "I left behind thirty books. 'Don't you think you are going to want those?'

my mother asked. 'Mama, I know what I'm doing,' I said. But she was right. I left behind D. H. Lawrence and I miss him already."

Nick was afraid she was going to go down the list of thirty books.

"Listen," said Nick, "I would really like to talk but this is kind of heavy and I am in a hurry. I have an appointment."

"Why didn't you say so?" she said, opening the door to her apartment, "you can leave it here till later."

At first Nick hesitated. Then he realized his good fortune. The incriminating evidence in her apartment. He would be free and clear. The police would never think of questioning her. She was truly innocent anyway and had no idea what Nick was giving her.

"Gee, that is really nice of you..." Nick said, groping for her name as he rested the carton in the corner behind the door.

"Lisa. I'm Lisa," she said, extending her hand. Nick and Lisa walked down the three flights together in lively chatter. They agreed to get together for drinks or dinner. She was young enough to be his daughter.

CHAPTER 42

November 30, 2004

THE NINTH PRECINCT IS a precinct like any other. Two tones of institutional blue paint, fluorescent lighting, some offices along the sides, a sergeant's booking desk in the middle. Slow day. Some banter between cops in uniform and plainclothes. Rather quiet and civilized, all things considered.

Officer Follanico appeared to greet Nick with an extended hand and a slap on the shoulder. He walked Nick over to an office in the back. There was a plaque, "Detective Leonard Cockburn." The door was open.

"Detective," said Officer Follanico, "dis is Mistuh Belladonna."

"Thank you, Officer Follanico," said Detective Cockburn. Formal yet friendly.

Cockburn was the typical detective: suspenders, sleeves rolled up, a nuts and bolts, no-nonsense kind of guy, not much of a sense of humor but a good person, a good cop. That was Nick's take. Hard-working, intelligent, incorruptible, courageous. A good family man, loyal to his wife, probably coached the local soccer team, and played catch with his kid in the backyard. He believed in the system and was one of the reasons the system almost seemed believable.

The two men shook hands.

"Call me Lenny," Detective Cockburn insisted. Nick really didn't want to, but realized he didn't have a choice.

They sat down across the desk from each other. Then, as if he had forgotten something very important, Detective Cockburn jumped up from his seat, walked over to a corner of the office, bent down and opened a small refrigerator.

"Root beer, 7-Up, Coke – regular and diet – Sprite. What'll it be?"

"I'll take a root beer," said Nick.

Detective Cockburn placed some ice in two glasses on his desk, opened the cans – Nick's first – and filled both of the glasses.

"Well, where do we begin?" he said, as he sat down.

Nick, of course, did not have the answer to that question and so said nothing. Cockburn had all the cards and he was going to play out his hand slowly and thoughtfully.

"All right," he said, pushing his glass of soda to one side and resting his forearms on the desk. "Here's what we have. Jeremiah Greenfield is dead. That is for sure. He is found hanging from a tree in Central Park. That is for sure. But here is where things stop adding up. Why would he come to Central Park to hang himself? I searched the records and couldn't find another single example. It's not like jumping off a bridge, there is plenty of that. But hanging yourself in Central Park? Nothing. Nada. That is part of the problem. No suicide note. Nada. No apparent motive. Let's say he wanted to make a political statement of some kind. All right. Where's the note or the symbol, the explanation? Remember those monks in Viet Nam? Self-immolation. They set themselves afire to protest a nasty war. But the whole world knew what they were doing and why. Here we have Mr. Greenfield hanging from a tree, and what for? Why didn't he just jump out his window? There has got to be something more."

Here he stopped short. Nick was caught up in his words and wasn't ready to respond. Lenny looked at him with strong, steady eyes, waiting for him to say something. Nick had what he wanted, that little piece of paper with the words "NO MORE LIES" written on it. But for some reason he couldn't tell him. Telling him and making the case for suicide would take the heat off Nick. But telling him would make him wonder why Nick hadn't come forward with the paper and what else he had or knew. One thing would lead to another. Nick would have a tough time lying to this guy.

"Anything there, Mr. Belladonna, that you want to tell me?"

Nick shook his head.

"What was he like those last days? What were the signs that he might have wanted to kill himself?"

"Well," Nick said, clearing his throat nervously. "Jeremiah was none too happy. The election was slipping away. He kept making mistakes."

"Mistakes? I don't know if that is the word I would use. He was doing well, extremely well, and then all of a sudden starts doing some very stupid things, almost as if he were trying to throw the election, as if that is what he was supposed to do all along."

Here again, Lenny stopped and gave Nick one of those long, hard stares of his.

"Was he upset that things had taken a turn for the worst?"

"Oh, yes, he was upset. Very upset. His whole life was built around the possibility of being president and for a moment he almost had it and then it slipped through his fingers. He had lost his interest in lying in print. His marriage had broken up. What was left for him? Not much."

"Did he have any plans, did he talk about anything?"

"When Jeremiah was down on his luck and depressed he got a bit grandiose. Once – after he was fired as editor –"

Lenny cut Nick off.

"He was fired? What was that about?"

"I don't know. I think the owner got tired of his line of nonsense."

"Who replaced him?"

"I did."

"You did? Walked right in over his warm body? Did you have anything to do with his getting fired?"

"I know what you're thinking and that's bullshit. I didn't want the job, screwed it up and almost got fired myself."

"If you didn't want it, why did you take it?"

"If I didn't take it I probably would have gotten fired anyway."

"But you almost did get fired."

"For different reasons."

"For different reasons," he repeated. "Did Jeremiah resent your moving in on his turf?"

"Nah, he understood," Nick said, avoiding Lenny's eyes.

"Did he?" Lenny persisted.

"I don't know. What's the difference?" Nick said. "Anyway, he started rambling."

"What about?"

"After he got fired he started rambling on about how he was going to write a letter to the president, explaining how the president could fight a war in the Middle East without shedding any blood."

"What did he ramble on about this time?"

"This time, it was a novel."

Nick stopped.

"Well, what was it about?"

"You want to hear the story?"

"Yes, I want to hear the story."

"He said he was going to make something up about a young dark-haired woman named Emily who walks with a limp. She lives with her mother and sister in a small town in Iowa and earns her living hand-lettering signs for local merchants. She has abilities as an artist that her overbearing mother has crushed.

"But she has dreams of studying art in Italy, and meeting a handsome, young Italian physician who has a villa overlooking the Mediterranean. He admires her art, is enraptured with her and pledges to devote himself to her and her career.

"Emily meets the man of her dreams, Antonio, on a two-week trip to Europe for which, unbeknownst to her mother, she had been scrimping and saving for eight years. She never returns to Iowa, abandoning some half-painted signs to her younger sister, Eileen, also an artist, and moves into the villa with Antonio.

"Emily paints some magnificent paintings, unlike anything she has done before, inspired by the beauty of the setting and Antonio's devotion. She lives in bliss for three years, has achieved ultimate fulfillment as an artist but is finding Antonio dull. He is mindlessly devoted to her. He lacks passion. He makes designs on the tablecloth with the tines of his fork after he has finished dinner and is drinking his coffee. Emily starts having affairs, first with the druggist, then with a traveling salesman. Finally, when Antonio finds out and refuses to give up on her, she poisons herself to death. There would be a great death scene."

"Let me ask you something," said Lenny out of the blue, "did you ever know anyone named Samantha Srongenson?"

Nick's face turned white. He swallowed hard and held his breath. The son of a bitch had set him up. Got him involved in narrating this stupid tale and then caught him completely off guard. He was good.

"Take a breath," said Lenny.

Nick took a breath.

"Now why don't you tell me about Ms. Srogenson."

There was no way Nick could lie now. Any lying would only make it worse. Nick told him about the phone call, the plane ride, Crispy's, missing Samantha, going out back, finding her propped up against the wall, going back inside, the hairy arm dropping the – Nick tried to catch himself but it was too late. The one thing he was not supposed to say, ever, he had started saying and couldn't take back. The note from Samantha. The one he had wanted to destroy.

"What did the note say?" asked Lenny.

"It said, 'Watch out. N.B.S.S.'"

"So Samantha was trying to warn Jeremiah about something or someone. What exactly do those initials mean?"

"I don't know. I tried figuring it out myself. It doesn't make any sense."

Lenny reached into his drawer and came out with a pen and a piece of paper.

"Write it down exactly as she wrote it."

Nick did as he was told. Lenny took the piece of paper. He studied it, took the pen, filled in some blanks and pushed the piece of paper back across the desk for Nick to read.

"Watch out for Nick Belladonna. Samantha Srongenson."

"Does that make any sense to you, Mr. Belladonna?" he asked. "Before you answer I want you to know something. I sent your name out over the wires. It seems that when the police searched Samantha's apartment they found a list of initials with names alongside. 'N.B.: Nick Belladonna.' They found a notebook with journal entries. There was one entry dated Friday, October 30, 2004 which said, 'Watch out for N.B.' What do you think?"

Nick took a long moment before answering. He had lost complete control of the situation. Everything he was saying and not saying was making him out to be a killer. He had never killed anyone. But here he was half-believing that he had, or at least feeling so hopelessly trapped that he had best admit to it anyway. He should have stopped and asked to speak to a lawyer, but didn't.

"Why was Samantha warning Jeremiah to watch out for you? Did she have reason to believe that you were going to kill him?"

"Kill him? Why the hell would I want to kill him? I was his best friend."

"Best friend? The same best friend who gets him fired and then takes his job. The same best friend who becomes his campaign manager and then sets him up to take a fall."

He knew a lot and had put enough of the pieces together to connect Nick to Jeremiah's undoing. Nothing Nick could say would have made things any worse.

"It's all about CRAP," Nick said in subdued tones.

"Crap, Mr. Belladonna? Don't toy with me."

"It's not crap," Nick corrected him, spelling out the letters. "It's CRAP, the Committee to Resurrect the American Presidency."

"What's CRAP got to do with it, Mr. Belladonna?" asked Lenny, leaning back in his chair and pushing out his lips in disgust.

Nick told him about wavy-haired Bob, the Ferrari, the apartment, the bank accounts, Jeremiah as the stalking-horse, Jeremiah who was too good and had to take a fall.

"Let me see if I get this straight," said Lenny. "You, Nicholas Belladonna, Jeremiah's best friend, were on the CRAP payroll to get Jeremiah to run and then take a fall so the incumbent could get reelected. Is that the way it goes?"

"That's the way it goes."

"And then things get out of hand. Jeremiah is too damned good. They have to get him out of the way, so they string him up from a tree in Central Park and try to make it look like a suicide. Is that how it goes?"

"Could be," Nick said resolutely.

"You have to rub out Samantha because she is about to blow the whistle."

"That's pure bullshit," Nick said, pounding the armrest. "Pure bullshit."

"Let me ask you this question," said Lenny in a quiet voice, leaning forward on the desk with his hands folded. "Isn't it true that if not for you, his best friend, Jeremiah would be alive today?"

Nick took in some air through his nose and then let it out, tapped his fingers nervously on the edge of the desk a few times.

"Yes," he said. "It's true."

"Mr. Belladonna," said Lenny rising from his chair to end the meeting, "don't go too far. I'm going to check out your Crispy crap story. It better hold."

Nick gave Lenny wavy-haired Bob's telephone number and

address and the location of Crispy's.

"These CRAP people play for keeps," Nick warned him. "You're never going to find out what happened."

"We'll see about that," Lenny said confidently.

CHAPTER 43

That Evening

NICK HEADED STRAIGHT FOR a bar on Second Avenue and 11th Street, a dive where you can get cheap Scotch and live blues. A blond with short hair, glasses and a nice belly button was singing her heart out. The bass notes were thumping up through the floor and against the side of his head. He ordered a double Scotch, gulped it down and then ordered a second.

He went over every detail of his conversation with Lenny. One sentence kept getting jumbled in his head and getting mixed up with other sentences. "Isn't it true that if not for you, his best friend, Jeremiah would be alive today?" Nick wanted to keep that sentence in his awareness all at once, grapple with its meaning, but the sentence kept slipping away. He finished the second double Scotch and ordered a third.

Jeremiah would be alive today. Yes, he would be alive today. If.

If a lot of things. If he hadn't been so damned good, for one thing. If he hadn't had this lifelong hang-up about being president of the United States, for another. If he hadn't been beat down by that son of a bitch father of his. If he hadn't married Emma. If he hadn't been a lying fraud for most of his life.

Nick ordered another double Scotch and downed it. Then, all of a sudden, things became clear. Indeed, Nick had killed Jeremiah, just as sure as if he had put the rope around his neck and looped it over that old elm tree. Lenny was dead right. If not for Nick, Jeremiah would still be alive.

Having settled that business in his head, Nick felt quiet inside but was finding the loud music more than he could take. He left the bar and walked down Second Avenue. He stopped at the first liquor store he could find and picked up a bottle of vodka. He walked downtown and then turned east on Tenth Street. He stepped into a doorway, unscrewed the cap, took a long swallow of vodka and then continued on his way. He took another few steps, slowed down for another swallow or two and then another few steps. By the time he was midway down the block he was halfway through the bottle. Here is where things got a little sketchy. Did Nick sit down on the sidewalk to finish the bottle or did he fall down – that would explain the cut lip and the blood on his shirt – and pass out? All he knew for sure was that he awoke sometime early in the morning – three or four – in the emergency room of Beth Israel Hospital. His clothes were covered with a mixture of vomit and blood. Standing at the end of the bed with a long face was Meghan.

"I am fine. Don't worry," Nick screamed. Except, no one heard him. That's because his lips weren't moving and his vocal chords were inert. No part of him was moving except for a little homunculus trapped inside who was frantically trying to get out. In fact, lying there, Nick thought that maybe he was dead and that this was what afterlife was like.

Nick must have passed out again. It was some time later or maybe the next day when he awoke again. This time he was in a different room with just one empty bed next to him. He had been scrubbed down and was scantily clad in a baby blue hospital gown. Everything about him felt fresh and clean. His lips were dried out. There was an IV in his arm.

A middle-aged black nurse from the Caribbean bustled in and fussed about.

"Now what you bin doin' carryin' on like dat for?" she asked in her beautiful sing-songy Caribbean way.

Nick just shook his head and gave a half-smile that hurt his lips.

"Dis afternoon we gettin' you outa bed an wheelin' you down to an AA meetin' see if we can knock some sense into dat head a yours."

Nick was too weak to protest and liked the idea of being pushed around and wheeled about.

As promised, at three o'clock he was transported to an AA meeting somewhere down in the bowels of the hospital. This was a ghastly collection of mutilated misfits. One fellow had a nasty-looking face and his right arm in a sling, probably a barroom brawl. Another had cracked lips and scabs up and down his arms. A young black with a goatee, muscular and relatively healthy-looking, was missing his right leg below the knee. There were about eight men not counting the leader, the only intact ambulatory one in the room, an outsider brought in to run the meeting.

The meeting began with the usual rigamarole and then the leader went around the room trying to get something out of each and every one of them. Nick was the last to go. On that particular day he felt bathed in a light of purity and innocence.

"My name is Nick. I'm an alcoholic," he said with aplomb and humility.

"Hi, Nick" came back the response.

The meeting ended and Nick was wheeled back to his room. The rest of the day passed peacefully. It was dinnertime when Detective Lenny Cockburn made an appearance. He came with flowers under his arm, which the nurse put in a vase. Lenny pulled up a chair and got right down to business.

"Your Crispy crap story checked out," he said. "Sorry I had to put you through that. I spoke to your friend, Bob. He couldn't have been more helpful. Told me how upset he had been about Jeremiah's death, about how depressed Jeremiah had been, how he had offered Jeremiah a job in his organization just to try and cheer him up, how Jeremiah was probably the kind of person this country needed to get it back on track. A really nice guy, your friend Bob."

Lenny was talking fast and smiling a lot. CRAP had scared the shit out of him.

CHAPTER 44

Time Passes

FOUR DAYS IN THE hospital and then Nick was off to Meghan's place in Yonkers. It was cozy and comfortable in the O'Toole household where Mother O'Toole ran a close second to Glenlivet. She was always on call, couldn't do enough. She insisted that Nick eat something. Maybe it was his appetite or her cooking, but the chemistry wasn't working. He did like her beef-and-barley soup, though, and she was an excellent baker.

By the end of a week, Nick was feeling stronger and decided it was time to pay a visit to the apartment at 57th Street. The place had to be cleaned out and closed down by the end of the December. Nick spent some time boxing what would be saved and throwing away the rest.

There were stacks of eight-by-ten photos capturing various moments in Jeremiah's campaign. There were some excellent shots of him on Long Island speaking to the potato farmers, in Flint, Michigan, speaking to unemployed auto workers. There was a great picture of him near the fountain in Bryant Park giving his "I'm a liar. Are you?" speech and another of his blowing his nose into the American flag.

Looking over the pictures, Nick realized there was a big hole in his life where Jeremiah used to be. He thought back to their days in the army. Those were their best times together. He remembered how good it felt to reconnect that day at Giacomos and how well they worked as a team when Jeremiah first started at the *Ledger*. Meghan was right. Jeremiah had trusted him and looked to him for guidance. How could he have betrayed him? What was he thinking? The burden of sadness would not go away.

Nick wasn't the only one who was sad to see Jeremiah go. Hardly a week had passed before publishing houses were vying with each other to come out with the first authorized biography. Myths and stories about Jeremiah multiplied. Little clans and groups sprouted up across the country organizing around what they thought he had stood for. There was the "League for Reformed Reporters," an organization for reporters who had "given up lying and chosen the truth." In a small town in Minnesota there was a group that called itself the "Coalition for True Democracy," which was trying to live out Jeremiah's bizarre proposal for "government by council." In a suburb of Atlanta there was a Bible-thumping preacher who had formed a sect basing its tenets on Jeremiah's recently discovered – which is to say, purely fabricated – religious writings, calling itself, "The Gospel According to Greenfield."

On May 1, 2005, six months to the day after Jeremiah's death by hanging, there was a memorial service in his honor. Just about anyone who is anyone was there, more than two thousand guests in all, honored and otherwise, seated in row after row stretching from 72nd Street to 61st Street along Poet's Walk where, fittingly, the ceremony was held. It was a perfect spring day.

Sissy was there with her new husband. Meryl and Barry Upshaw were there. The cleaning lady was there. Maynard was there with his wife, carrying his new baby in a sling across his chest. Some homeless people were there, though not by invitation. Meghan was there with Mother O'Toole and Kelly. Emma was there, overflowing in every direction, wearing flower-patterned slacks that did not fit and a blouse that was popping its buttons. CRAP was conspicuous in its absence.

There was an orchestra and a chorus that began the event with a moving rendition of "The Battle Hymn of the Republic." There were quotes from the Bible, the Declaration of Independence, Thomas Jefferson and Thomas Paine.

The service began in earnest with a eulogy by the president.

"We have lost a great American," he began in a voice filled with sadness, "an American who was great not because he was rich, or because he was powerful, but because he fought for what he believed in, fought with persistence and dignity, not for reward or recognition, but because he cared."

The president seemed genuinely moved by his own words.

"Jeremiah Greenfield cared about people, small people, people who are struggling to find peace and fulfillment in life. But most of all, he cared about his country. He cared about this great land of ours."

The president made a sweeping gesture with his left hand.

"Jeremiah Greenfield understood what it meant to be an American. He understood that we are a country with a proud political heritage, that we are devoted to the simple virtues, virtues like freedom, justice and truth, and that this is where our greatness lies."

Here the president left behind his notes and seemed to be speaking from memory, or else making it up as he went along.

"In the history of civilization, only one country was founded on political beliefs, fashioning itself into existence out of the driving wish to see to it that this would be a land of liberty and the pursuit of happiness, where the rights of each and every individual would be secured and guaranteed. Our fervent belief in these inalienable rights, this is what America brings to the world. This is where she is a leader and an inspiration to people everywhere, especially to

211

those living under the iron fist of tyranny. We are their only hope and we must not forget them."

There was a hush, filled with bird song and a radio blasting in the distance.

"But how can we do this most important job for everyone else, securing the rights of freedom and justice – a job more critical to the world's survival than bombs and bullets, space walks, and fast-moving cars – if we cannot do it for ourselves?"

The president grabbed the lectern with both hands and searched the crowd with his eyes. His voice was tense with emotion.

"For if but one poor soul sleeps under a piece of cardboard on a park bench, is that justice in America?

"If but one artist is afraid to speak the truth, is that freedom in America?

"If an elite of power-hungry oligarchs runs the country," he said, completely forgetting himself, "is that democracy in America?"

Now he became calmer. His voice was subdued.

"A human being has taken his life. Let us not look back a week, a month, a year or more from now and say, 'Oh. What a shame. What a waste.' No, that would be terrible. That would be too great a tragedy. We must not allow his heroic act to be dishonored through cowardice or indifference. We must struggle for that truth, that justice, that he hoped by his death we would come to once again appreciate. We must honor him with our loyalty to all he believed, for in honoring him, we honor ourselves and this great land we live in."

The president ended to a solemn hush. Not a sound could be heard, save the rustling of leaves and the music of the spheres. It was by common consent his greatest speech, and his biggest lie.

ABOUT THE AUTHOR

ARTHUR D. ROBBINS is a psychologist with a practice on Manhattan's Upper West Side. He holds a doctorate in psychology from New School University and a doctorate in French and Roman Philology from Columbia University where he specialized in 18th century political thought. From Voltaire he learned that humor and politics can be brought together in a work of fiction. Currently, Dr. Robbins is working on his next novel.